Twist of Fate

This book is dedicated to the all the families that lost loved ones in the deadly tornadoes that swept through Alabama, Mississippi and Missouri in 2011.

Chapter 1

"God damn it, Vega, find me a fucking road." Remy Tate shouted. She leaned over the steering wheel and stared through the windshield at the menacing looking sky overhead. "We're gonna lose it!"

"Chill, Chica." Carmen Vega said sarcastically. "The storm hasn't even dropped a funnel yet." Carmen squinted at the smart phone in one hand and the wrinkled map in the other. Her long brown hair was pulled back in a ponytail. Her chocolate brown eyes were hidden behind Raybans, despite the fact that the clouds had made it look almost like night outside. Her perpetually brown skin glistened with sweat, her Puerta Rican heritage belying the fact that she spent a lot of time in a car and not actually out in the sun. At forty—one, she was well past the age that she gave a shit what anyone thought about her. She lived too many years to be stuck doing something she hated. That's why when her best friend Remy had begged her to be her spotter, she jumped at the chance for a new adventure. So far, each new tornado season had given her enough excitement to stay and the stops in between had given her enough female companionship to make it enjoyable. "Take a right here. We should pick up County Road 250 South. We can take it all the way out to North 4 and intersect with the storm near Meriden."

Remy ran a hand through her dirty blond hair and fixed her hazel eyes on Carmen. "You're sure? I don't want to miss another one." Carmen had gotten them lost on the last chase, and they missed a storm that dropped five tornadoes, including one that was an EF4. What made it even worse, was Remy's biggest competition in the field of storm chasing, Sarah Phillips, had been caught in an EF2 tornado and sold the footage to CNN. It was the first time anyone had ever ridden a tornado and it infuriated Remy that it hadn't been her team that was involved. She had cussed at Carmen for two hours straight and had it been anyone but Carmen, they would have caught the first greyhound and left Remy by herself, shit out of luck. "Just making sure. Hell of a storm we missed."

Carmen rolled her eyes. "Listen, Chica, you keep riding my ass about that and you're gonna be driving with one hand and reading the map by your damn self."

"Promises, promises. I couldn't get rid of you if I tried." Remy slowed and turned right on County Road 250 South. The dust flew up around them and mixed with the tiny droplets of water on the windshield. She tried running the wiper blades over it, but all that succeeded in doing was streaking the dirt around further. "How far away are we?"

Carmen squinted at the map, comparing it to the storms developing just northeast of them. "I'm guessing five miles." She glanced out the window at the clouds whirling around them. "Maybe ten, tops."

Remy pushed the pedal down a bit more, nursing as much out of Thor as she could. Thor, as she had named the Dodge Ram that was incased in a layer of thin steel, jumped almost imperceptively and the speedometer needle edged up slightly. It wasn't the most attractive ride and could almost be confused with a wartime tank, but it was by far the safest mode of transport to face the danger of the tornadoes and other weather they faced almost daily. During the tornado season, they could track a dangerous storm most days even if it meant spending countless hours driving from one dying storm to the next, sometimes existing on only a few hours' sleep. "How's it looking so far?"

Carmen held the radar up in front of Remy's face and watched a small smirk form in the corner of her mouth. She could see from the radar a small bow echo had already formed in the squall line, and that meant they had a pretty good chance of seeing at least one funnel cloud, and maybe a tornado would drop, if they were lucky. "Looks good, Chica, no?"

Remy's only response was a slight nod. She didn't waste much time on chit chat. That had been a complaint of her girlfriends in the past. She never talked or at least not enough for them. She didn't spend a lot of time gushing about her feelings either. She figured if the woman she was with needed constant reassurance, she was with the wrong girl. In her relatively short time on the earth, she hadn't met a woman that she was willing to change for. But hell, twenty—nine was old enough that she didn't care if she ever changed.

She concentrated on the road in front of her. The rain was coming down in sheets now, and she was having a hard time making out the lanes between the heavy drops. She could just make out the shelf cloud now not more than five miles away. Her heart started to beat faster. Chasing storms was like sex to her. Seeing the storm develop, watching for rotation, flying down country roads in search of the next storm were all like foreplay to her. The tornado dropping and watching the massive storm rage across the land, sometimes running in the opposite direction was like an orgasm.

Her body hummed in anticipation. She could tell the temperature had dropped from the earlier highs, but she could still feel the sweat coat her body. She felt a rush building deep inside her and she smiled. It was her drug. She was addicted to this. She glanced sideways at Carmen and saw the telltale vessel bulging in her neck. They would get one today. Remy knew better than to ignore Carmen's intuition. Aside from the one time they had gotten lost, Carmen hadn't let her down. Her uncanny ability to sense where the most active storm systems would develop had gotten them close to the danger more times than not.

Through the open window, she could smell the storm, and it teased her baser self. Her feral sense heightened like a hunter tuned into its prey. She could feel it in her blood. "Wall cloud." Remy said almost to herself.

Carmen leaned forward and followed Remy's finger. She could see the dark edge of the storm, and she looked for rotation. This was the pattern every time. Carmen guiding the two in haphazard fashion. No fancy monitors displaying the latest radars from local weather stations, only her smart phone and a handheld map. They didn't rely on GPS, only her uncanny ability to read a map and sense the danger.

Remy watched the sky, absentmindedly biting her fingernails. She slowed the truck to a crawl and pulled a small video camera from behind her and started taping. She jumped when the first chunk of hail hit the outside of their steel hull. She angled the truck, hoping that the pieces wouldn't hit at a bad angle and crack or worse yet, break through the windshield. She could feel the rain stinging her bare arm and resisted rolling up the window. She'd had hail break through the window before and having to go to the doctor to get the glass removed from her eye was not something she cared to repeat anytime soon. "There!" She shouted.

Carmen squinted and just made out the thin rope twister spiraling towards the ground. "Tornado! Tornado. I see debris. We have confirmed touchdown." She dialed the phone. When the 911 operator picked up, she identified herself. "This is Carmen Vega. I'm a storm chaser. We are just southwest of Meriden. We have a confirmed tornado spotting. Repeat, confirmed touchdown on Highway 4, just southwest of Meriden."

Remy pulled a Nikon camera from behind her and handed it to Carmen. "Get some still shots. It's a small one, probably not more than an EF1."

Carmen shook her head. "Let's head further east. The storm looks like it's intensifying and there's a supercell forming over Oskaloosa."

Remy looked around her. "And, how am I supposed to get there genius? Last I checked, 4 only runs north—south, and you want me to go dead east? I'll have to run all the way back down to 237 and come back up. The storm will be long gone by then."

Carmen smiled crookedly. "How daring are you feeling Chica?"

Remy shot her a look as if to say what crazy mess are you about to get me into. "Not sure yet, how daring do you want me to be?"

"Mmm, I've got some suggestions." Carmen winked suggestively. "But, I don't think you could handle a brown girl."

Remy snorted loudly. "Oh yeah? You think you're Puerto Rican blood is too much for me?"

"Dios mio." Carmen said loudly. "You are just a baby, I would break you."

"I've handled more than a hot—blooded Latina, so don't get too big a head." Remy said sarcastically. "Now, what's the plan?"

Carmen took one more glance at the map and pointed north. "Take 4 another mile or so. We'll run into 92. We should be able to take that straight across."

Remy's brow furrowed. "Drive straight under the storm? Across Perry Lake? You are crazier than I thought."

"You want action then do it. If you want to be a pussy, fine we'll settle for an EF1 today." Carmen shrugged. "I'm sure I could come up with something to keep us busy if you want to be a chicken shit."

Remy gunned the truck and dirt shot out behind them. She muttered softly. "You are loco."

"Loca." Carmen corrected. "Gotta use the feminine. I'm all lady remember."

Remy rolled her eyes. "Yeah, and I'm a virgin." She slowed and turned east on 92. She shot Carmen a look. "You sure about this? I mean I know I'm game, but a *lady* like yourself might get scared."

"Keep it up, Chica. You'll be more afraid of the storm inside the car than the one you're chasing." Carmen glanced out the window. The few trees that bordered the lake were almost horizontal from the high winds of the storm. She could see the choppy waves of Perry Lake and knew that they were nearing the eye of the storm. "We're close. Another couple of miles, and we will be right underneath her."

"Been in that situation before." Carmen teased. "Right underneath a writhing, wet storm. Mmm—mmmm, wouldn't mind that right now."

Remy snorted. Carmen ate, slept and breathed sex. Her Latina blood flowed with sensuality and she very rarely spent her nights alone. She loved women, and she loved making love to them. If the screams coming from the hotel room next to hers were any indication, Remy knew she didn't just love it, she was very accomplished at pleasing women. "Look, there it is. Shit. That's a massive supercell."

"We've got a giant hook echo." Carmen said quietly. No matter how many times they had seen this, it never failed to amaze her. The fact that the environment could produce a storm that was so awe—inspiring, and yet so destructive at the same time, still made her breath catch. "Definite rotation."

Remy slowed down again and her eyes concentrated on the dark clouds overhead. "There!" She shouted. "Funnel. It's starting. See it?"

Carmen nodded. She pointed the video camera at the growing funnel cloud. "I got it, I got it!"

Remy pulled the truck over, the winds from the storm whipping it around mercilessly even though it weighed several tons. Her heartbeat sped up, and her breathing became more rapid. "It's dropping." She pointed excitedly. "There it is." She snapped picture after picture. "God, it's massive. It has to be over a quarter of a mile wide."

"Oh shit." Carmen jumped. She could make out sparks in the distance as the tornado ripped through the flat farmland and pulled up power lines, causing them to spark wildly. "It's coming this way."

Remy's heart pounded. The tornado had turned and was barreling down on them. She threw the truck into drive and gunned the engine. She fixed her eyes on the road and tried to steal glances at the tornado. It seemed like it was moving much faster than they were, and she shoved the pedal to the floor, coaxing a few more horsepower out of the already taxed engine. "Shit, shit, shit!" Her escalating voice got lost in a rumble of thunder.

"Vamos, Chica." Carmen's body was rigid, her hand tight on the door handle. "We've got to go faster." Normally, she didn't get frightened, but the now half—mile tornado was barreling down on them.

Remy slowed enough to take the sharp turn onto 59 and started heading south. She could hear the annoying sound of the weather siren peeling through the truck speakers. *The National Weather Service has issued a…"*

"It's official." Carmen shrugged. "They're only five minutes behind this time." She watched the spinning mass in her side mirror. She saw large pieces of debris swirling up the tornado wall and shooting out the sides. "If it stays on course, it should miss Oskaloosa."

"Thank God." Remy swore in exasperation. It's gotta be EF3, maybe EF4. It would level the town." She breathed a sigh of relief when the truck finally gained some distance on the tornado. She slowed down and turned the truck in as tight a circle as possible so they could watch the tornado's path out of the line of danger.

They watched it rage across the plain for several more minutes before it started to shrink and eventually pulled back into the clouds above. Remy wiped the sweat off her face. "Shit, that was close."

Carmen shook her head. "I got some kick ass footage though. I think that's our best one yet."

Remy nodded in agreement. "That little brush with death has got me jonesing for a beer. Point me in the direction of the nearest bar."

Remy followed 59 south towards the small town of Lawrence. They were in between Topeka and Kansas City, and she could have opted for either one, but the rush and the stress of running from the tornado had worn her out, and all she wanted was a beer and a soft bed.

Twenty minutes later, she pulled into the parking lot of the Motel 6.

"Really?" Carmen sighed. "Motel 6?"

Remy opened the door and got out, ignoring Carmen's comment. "I'll get us a room."

Chapter 2

Remy pulled into the parking lot of Johnny's Tavern and sighed loudly. "The room is fine, you baby."

Carmen snorted loudly. "I know at least one cockroach crawled across my luggage, and that was before I even set it down on the floor."

"So, take the car." Remy opened her door and headed towards the bar, ignoring the string of expletives that Carmen was hurling at her in Spanish. She propped the door open with her foot and stood waiting, her arms akimbo. "You coming sometime tonight?"

Carmen flipped her the bird as she walked past, choosing not to respond to Remy's snide comment. "Come on, Chica, let's just get our drink on."

"I couldn't have said it better myself." Remy followed Carmen into the bar and weaved her way through the tables to a table near the back. Her eyes were fixed on the corner, and she didn't see Carmen stop abruptly, causing her to run smack into Carmen's back. "Jesus, Vega. What the fuck?"

Carmen pointed towards an occupied table in the opposite corner and smiled wickedly. "Sorry. I couldn't help myself. That is one muy bonita Chica in the corner. I don't know about you, but that's where I'm drinking my beer tonight."

Remy followed her gaze and nearly came out of her boots. "I'll be damned!" She followed Carmen to the table and smiled down at the two occupants, waiting for them to acknowledge the new visitors.

Sarah Phillips met Remy's bemused gaze and groaned. "Remy."

"What's up, Bonneville?" Remy smirked and sidestepped a fist flying towards her stomach. "Mind if we join you?"

"Actually, yes, I do mind." Sarah's voice was curt, but not rude. "We've got a lot to discuss and I don't need the competition sitting around stealing ideas."

"It's okay, Chica." Carmen put her hand on Remy's shoulder and pushed her a step back. "Buenos noches, senoritas. Forgive my pushy partner. She hasn't learned, the how you say manners yet." Carmen's accent, which was barely evident in every day conversation was thick tonight. She was obviously hoping to win Sarah and her companion over with her charm. "We didn't mean to bother you, and if you prefer to not have our company, we will be happy to sit elsewhere."

"Come on, Cuz, what's one night going to hurt?" Sarah's cousin, Parker Kennedy, turned her baby blues towards Carmen and shot her a smile. "Hi, I'm Parker…Kennedy. How do you know my cousin?"

Carmen shook her outstretched hand in a firm handshake, then let her fingers linger a moment longer than someone with no interest would. "Carmen Vega. I haven't had the pleasure of *officially* meeting, what was your name, Bonneville? Only Rem's had that honor." She watched Remy expectantly.

"Sarah Phillips, the illustrious Carmen Vega." Remy waited while they said hello then leaned behind Carmen and shook Parker's hand. "Remy Tate. Nice to meet you." She pulled back and grabbed Carmen's arm. "Come on, let's get out of here."

14

Parker grabbed Carmen's hand and stopped them. "Come on, you guys. Sit down. Sarah doesn't mind, do you, Sarah?"

Sarah rolled her eyes. She hadn't ever been able to say no to Parker and it seemed tonight wouldn't be the first time. She motioned at the empty chairs and smiled. "Sure, whatever."

Remy sat down wearily, the day's events taking a toll on her mentally and physically. No matter how much she enjoyed the chase, it always wore her out. Her gaze met Sarah's and she smiled a cute sideways smile. She wrapped a light brown curl around her forefinger. "You got your hair cut since I saw you last. It's cute."

"Don't." Sarah whispered, her blue eyes blazing. "It won't work this time."

Remy flashed her an innocent smile. "What?"

"You know what I mean." Sarah said sternly. "Don't think you're going to act all cute and it's going to get you anywhere this time."

"What do you mean, it's not going to get me anywhere?" Remy asked innocently, but her eyes sparkled mischievously. She leaned in closer and whispered in Sarah's ear. "You mean back in your bed?"

Sarah's face turned five shades of red. "Yes. Whatever that was between us was a one—time thing. No amount of tricks is going to make me repeat that mistake."

"Tricks?" Remy asked. "If I remember correctly, there were no tricks, and you seemed to enjoy yourself as much as I did."

"Ooh!" Sarah groaned. "You never change."

"Nope." Remy was beaming. She grabbed a menu and opened it. "So, what's good here besides the beer?"

Parker picked that moment to pull her attention away from Carmen, where it had been since they sat down. "Try the calzone. You won't regret it."

Remy waived a waitress down and ordered two more pitchers and a calzone for herself and a salad for Carmen. She handed the menus back. "Thanks."

Parker laughed and covered Carmen's hand with hers. "You always let her order?"

Carmen laughed. "Have too. I'm trying to diet and if I order myself, I'd be eating a large pizza. Helps to have someone take charge…outside of the bedroom I mean." She winked at Parker.

"I can think of better ways to burn extra calories." Parker quipped. "And, besides, I like your curves."

"Seriously, Parker?" Sarah shot her a look. "They just got here."

Parker shrugged and ran a hand through her short hair. Her blue eyes twinkled. "Hey, you can't blame a girl for trying to get some in this God forsaken hick town out in the middle of nowhere."

"So, Sarah, what's up with Bonneville? Interesting nickname." Carmen teased. "Is that something we all get to use, or it that reserved for someone special?"

"Actually, it's my middle name. I made the mistake of telling *someone* that and she hasn't forgotten." Sarah took a swig of her beer and shot Remy a threatening look. "And, I prefer that she not call me that."

"But, did you tell her why that was your middle name?" Parker asked. "Something like that could only happen to my cousin."

Carmen poured herself a beer and leaned forward. "So, what's the story?"

"Nothing super exciting." Sarah sighed. "My mom was in labor with me and by the time she and my dad figured out she was in labor and left for the hospital, it was too late. They didn't make it on time and she ended up having me in the front seat of their 1971 Pontiac Bonneville. I've been living with that crazy name ever since."

"Guess you oughta be glad they didn't drive an Edsel."
Carmen laughed and Sarah couldn't help but laugh with her.
Her personality was infectious and the Spanish lilt in her
words made her incredibly sexy and appealing to anyone
around her.

"So, where's Evan?" Remy asked nonchalantly. She
didn't mind the scenery change, but Parker had her
wondering where Sarah's old partner was.

A cloud passed over Sarah's face. "Gone." She didn't
elaborate, and Remy could tell from her tone that whatever
had happened between the two of them had not been pretty.

She paused while the waitress set plates in front of them
and took a hearty bite of her calzone. "Ow, shit. That's hot."
She glared at Carmen, who was laughing out loud.

"Serves you right, Chica." She teased. "It's your
punishment for getting to eat the fattening foods while I'm
stuck munching on roughage."

"I bet I could take your mind off your diet." Parker
teased. A big flirt anyway, she was smitten with Carmen, and
it made her a hundred times worse.

"Really?" Sarah groaned. "I'm trying to eat here."

What?" Parker feigned innocence. "I'm merely
ascertaining the status of our guest's mental health and trying
to accommodate her discomfort."

"Okay, now I think I might throw up." Remy confessed.
She turned to Carmen. "Can you try to be a bit less
charming…at least while we eat."

"Si, Chica, no worries. I'm sorry, Parker. I'll try to be
disagreeable."

"I don't think you can." Parker winked. "Besides, we're
all adults here, and if I want to occupy myself with a little
extracurricular activity in my free time, you'll just have to
deal with it. I can't help it you took a vow of celibacy."

Sarah groaned. "God, it's going to be a long night."

"So, Remy, you never said how you knew my cousin."
Parker's eyes twinkled. She could tell from Sarah's response

to Remy's sudden appearance that they had history of some sort. She knew Sarah's recent swearing off of sex was directly related to Evan, although much to her chagrin, she didn't know the details. Her cousin had never been forthcoming with her love life, or lack thereof, and she was beginning to wonder if there wasn't a skeleton in Sarah's closet that resembled Remy. "Is there a nasty little scandal in your past?"

Sarah felt her cheeks starting to heat up and hoped it wasn't visible in the dim lights of the bar. She started to answer, but Remy saved her.

"Nothing exciting like that. We've run into each other on the circuit for a few seasons now." She wasn't sure that explanation sounded believable. She figured Parker would push, but she didn't. She at least pretended to buy the little white lie…thankfully. "Honestly, she's been my biggest competition yet. Never met anyone that could pick a spot with nothing happening and somehow make a storm out of it."

Parker scoffed. "You wouldn't have thought so today."

"How's that?" Remy asked. "You aren't losing your touch are you? You finally gonna let me get some CNN—worthy footage."

"No!" Sarah waggled her finger at Remy. "Just had an off day." Regret flashed in her eyes.

Remy leaned her body into Sarah's, her brow furrowed. She glanced at Carmen and Parker, satisfied they were wrapped up in each other she whispered. "Want to talk about it?"

"No." Sarah shook her head. "Nothing to talk about really. Just one of those days."

"Hmm." Remy searched her face. "Look, I know you are still ticked at me for that night, but can't we try to get past that? You look like you could use a friend. And, I know Parker isn't your therapist, because you don't ever talk to anyone."

"I'm not mad at you." Sarah confessed. "I'm frustrated with myself because that night was just another in a string of bad judgment calls. The latest was with Ev…" She stopped before she said Evan's name, but she could tell from the look on Remy's face she knew exactly what she was talking about. "I'm great at reading the weather, just not so great at reading people."

"You know I'm not a bad guy." Remy smiled ruefully. "I'm sorry that one night messed up a potentially good friendship. I like hanging out with you. I gotta get a break from Vega sometimes."

Carmen heard her name and pulled her gaze away from Parker's lips. "What?"

Remy shook her head. "Nothing, just saying what a treat it is to have you on the road with me."

Carmen smiled widely. "You lying sack of shit. I know when you're badmouthing me."

"Nah, just messing with you." Remy teased. "Go back to your date."

Carmen winked and turned back to Parker, who was so far lost in her eyes that she didn't respond at all to the conversation or she would have surely come to Carmen's defense.

Sarah smiled at Remy. "I enjoy your company too, and as much as I love Parker, it is nice to see a different face once in a while. Friendship is fine, just don't think because we are all buddy, buddy that I'm going to start spilling my life to you." She lowered her voice. "You know me more intimately than most people and that makes it really hard to open up to you, okay?"

"Fair enough, Bonneville." Remy poured another beer for herself and held the pitcher up to Sarah, with a questioning look in her eyes.

"Half a glass." Sarah said. "It's going to be an early morning tomorrow. I think we are headed towards Oklahoma City. I've got a feeling something's brewing there."

Remy smiled. "Good luck, Bonneville. We're heading the opposite direction. See you in a couple of weeks...in one piece, I hope."

Chapter 3

"Come on!" Sarah threw her hands up in exasperation. The storms that were predicted to impact parts of Eastern Oklahoma had yet to produce more than rain and some small hail. "There's gotta be something brewing."

She and Parker had made the trek from Kansas to Oklahoma City and were stalking the storm from the shelter of a Seven—Eleven. Parker slurped her frozen Mt. Dew loudly and shot Sarah a look. "We should have just stayed another day in Kansas."

Sarah rolled her eyes. "Carmen wasn't staying, you know. They were headed up to Iowa and South Dakota. Something about a line of storms that would put ours to shame."

"Well, looks like they may have hit on something." She showed Sarah the bright reds and yellows populating much of Eastern South Dakota and Northwestern Iowa. "Lot more going on there than in good old Oklahoma, *where the winds go sweeping 'cross the plains.*" Parker's voice peaked in a painful crescendo.

"Really? You're a lesbian. We don't do musicals." Sarah groaned. "Not only amazingly off—key, but amazingly embarrassing." She pushed Parker through the door to the parking lot. "We are leaving now."

Parker's laughter echoed out the door. "Yes, finally. Let's go chase something. Stop sitting around here sulking 'cause we aren't hanging with our girls."

"Sulking?" Sarah slammed the car door and waited for Parker to get in. "The only one sulking here is you, and you're just mad because you couldn't hook up last night."

Parker started the car. "Maybe. But, you gotta admit, she is so sexy. Even you would want her…that is if you weren't hung up on Remy."

"What!" Sarah shouted. "I am most certainly not hung up on Remy. I'm not…I'm not even attracted to her." She stammered the words out, not even sure why she was justifying the comment with an answer. It didn't matter whether she was attracted to her or not. Which obviously she wasn't, right? She hadn't succumbed to her charms…at least not a second time. No, she wouldn't make that mistake again. Although, she thought, at the time, it didn't feel like a mistake. It actually topped her short list of great sex, maybe even fantastic. *Stop it! It wasn't that great.* Sarah rubbed her eyes. *Oh, who are you kidding? It was amazing.*

"Uh—huh." Parker snickered. She watched the emotions play on her cousin's face and she thought for a second time, with more certainty now, that there was something between her and Remy. If not now, then at least sometime in the past. Curiosity was getting the better of her, but she sensed that now would not be the time that Sarah would decide to let her start playing Dr. Phil. "Glad we got that all straightened out. So, now can we go chase something?"

Sarah opened her mouth to say something, to keep protesting the subtle innuendoes that Parker was dropping here and there, but thought better of it. Somewhere in her mind, she heard Shakespeare. *Me thinks thou dost protest too much.* She shook her head. "Yeah, fine, let's go wrangle us a tornado."

"Wahoo." Parker yelled. "Saddle up, cowboy."

Sarah's eyes scanned the horizon. "It is getting darker. What do you think? Head south?"

Parker leaned into the radar, squinting at the changing color patterns. "I'll say. I'm picking up some rotation just southwest of Caddo. Moving northeast at thirty—five miles an hour. So, you better hurry."

Sarah hit the gas and the car surged forward with quick nimbleness. "God, I miss Bessie." Her mind flashed briefly to Evan. When they had split up, the truck had gone with Evan, since she had been the one that bought it. Now they were stuck driving around in her 2005 Chevy Caprice. Heavy yes, gaudy even more so, but a safe choice to chase tornadoes in? Not hardly, but up till now, the little bit of income they made selling videos to local stations, and the rare bigger storm that made them a little extra, there wasn't much left over for luxuries like girding a diesel truck with a steel skeleton. No, that was reserved for trust fund babies like Evan. Maybe, just maybe, with a successful season, her new employer, *Rogue Weather,* would outfit her with something better.

"God, I don't know why you named her that? Ten tons of steel and that's the best you could come up with." Parker pulled her ball cap off and ran her fingers through her spiked hair. "You know Chevy Chase is the perfect chasing car. Bet you're glad you let me name her."

"We are not the Griswolds, and we are totally not driving across the plains with your dead grandmother in the car." Sarah groaned.

"Real nice Clark, real nice." Parker teased. "Duly noted. No dead grandmothers in the Chevy Chasemobile."

Sarah saw a sign welcoming them to Tushka, Oklahoma. Population 347. "Let's park it here for a moment. Something's about to happen." She reached around behind her and grabbed the video camera and tripod. Her right ear was itching. Her tell that the storm was about to get crazy.

She opened the door and set the tripod up facing the southwest. "Get the camera."

Parker joined her on the hood of the car. The wind had started to whip up around them, sending bits of dirt swirling around them. "Hell of a shelf cloud. I'm seeing some rotation there."

Sarah followed her finger and smiled. She could smell the storm, and the scent went right through her body. She had not originally set out to be a storm chaser, but as a new meteorologist fresh out of school, she took the crap assignments. Going out to the field, interviewing the witnesses. It was on such an assignment eight years ago that she had first met Remy. She was young and reckless and so charming and thought she was hot shit. It was her enthusiasm for chasing the perfect storm that had bitten Sarah in the first place.

It was the summer of 2003 and a line of storms had produced tornadoes from Minnesota down to Oklahoma. Remy had gotten video footage of the worst one, an EF4. Sarah knew from the minute she met Remy that she was self—assured bordering on cocky, and sexy as hell. Having come from a small town, there weren't many other lesbians she got to interact with, and she had been so serious in college that she had only had one serious girlfriend and only slept with two women total.

Remy on the other hand, had traveled all over and given her dangerous career, likely had a girl in every town. She was wildly attractive with her somber, wide—set hazel eyes and full sensuous lips framed in a square face. Her blond hair was always unkempt and grazed her collar, no matter if she had just had a haircut or not. She was tall, her muscled lankiness giving her the appearance of a swimmer. In truth, she just had a high metabolism and honestly, if asked, couldn't tell you the last time she had eaten, too busy chasing the next storm.

It had been a night much like last night. Remy, fresh off a chase, laid back and comfortable and oozing too much sex appeal for a small town girl like Sarah to resist. They had fallen into bed together, and it was only as she lay awake, long after Remy had dozed off, that the first tendrils of regret had started to seep into her subconscious. Now, it was brief moments of regret, mingled with the awareness of learning from her mistakes, that occupied her mind in unguarded moments when she forgot to keep the memory in her past.

A shout brought her out of her reverie. "Look!" Parker shouted. "Funnel cloud, and it's growing fast."

Sarah watched with fascination on her face. No matter how many times she had seen this, it still amazed her. Even more so, she was amazed that with as much technology and time spent chasing and studying tornadoes, they really didn't know much more about them now than they had a hundred years ago. They were as unpredictable and sometimes as dangerous as people themselves and yet somehow, even with the danger they presented, she felt safer with storms than she did with most people.

"It's down, it's down." Parker danced excitedly. "There's a second funnel. Just left of the first, smaller but it's down, it's down too."

Before they could even realize what happened, the two twisters had merged into one larger tornado.

"Think we're safe here?" Parker asked loudly, yelling over the deafening roar.

"Yeah, yeah, we're fine." Sarah watched the tornado track across the flat land. "I think it's staying west of us."

They watched it grow till it was at least a quarter of a mile wide. "Oh shit." Sarah swore softly. "We're losing it. It's rain wrapped, it's rain wrapped. We gotta move!"

They jumped into the car and peeled out, headed north on Highway 69 towards Tushka. Sarah watched the storm out the window, straining to see the tornado through the rain.

When they finally hit a clearing, she gasped out loud. "It's heading straight for the town."

Parker strained to hear tornado sirens, but if they were going off, the sound was lost in the wind. "Oh God."

Sarah slammed the breaks on the car and watched stone—faced as the tornado cut straight through Tushka. "Oh, my God! Oh, my God."

They watched as it cut a swath through the center of town, hitting several buildings and sending debris flying through the air. The storm was massive. She guessed the winds to be somewhere near 150 mph, making it an EF3. She saw huge pieces of brick flying through the air, tossed like grains of sand.

"Oh man, I hope no one was in there." Parker said somberly. She flinched when she heard a sound like a shotgun resonate through the car. "What the fuck?"

"Hail." Sarah sounded scared. "And, from the sound of it, it's big." She glanced out the window. "Start praying Chevy Chase holds up."

Parker saw the chunks of hail now scattered around her. They were easily the size of golf balls and if one hit directly on the glass around them, they were screwed. An onslaught of gunshot peels rang out on the metal surrounding them as the hail picked up. "Okay, seriously, this needs to stop now. I'm freaking out a little."

"Tell me about it." Sarah agreed. She prayed the danger around them would leave her and Parker untouched, and that anyone in the small town being ravaged right now would survive. Her mind wandered back to her childhood. The funny thing is she had been afraid of storms as a child, hated them actually. She always hid in the bathroom anytime one came through, convinced that she wouldn't survive the fury outside. She did survive every time though, and by the time she met Remy, she was ready for a new adventure. She wanted more than just a one night stand, but it was a start.

She had been bitten by the bug and there was no turning back.

She came to when the intense pounding stopped and turned to Parker who was regarding her quizzically. "Still with me?"

"No, yeah, I'm here." Sarah laughed. "I think the worst is over. We need to go in and see if everyone is okay." She started the car and said a silent thank you that they had survived another storm. She had made it only a mile before she was forced to stop.

"Holy shit!" Parker swore loudly. "We aren't getting any closer than this." The highway was littered with overturned semis. Trees that had the tops violently wrenched off lay scattered about. If they wanted to survey the town, they were going to have to do it on foot.

They grabbed their cameras and flashlights, threw parkas on, and started towards the city. They were only a mile outside the city, but having to traverse the highway strewn with debris was going to take them awhile. "It's gonna get dark fast, we better put down tracks."

Parker nodded and cinched her parka closer around her body. The wind had died down, but the temperatures had dropped with the storm and there was a chill in the air.

They walked with no words, the somberness of the surrounding area dictating long moments of silence. Parker snapped pictures of the devastation along the way. The closer they got, the more litter was scattered about the road, and by the time they hit the city limits nothing could have prepared them for what they saw.

Even in the waning daylight, the scene in front of them took their breath away. Cars were upended, whole buildings lay in rubble on the ground. "We need to find a sheriff and make sure everyone's okay."

"Come on, that looks like the center of town." Parker gestured with her head. "The courthouse is still intact."

They passed a sign along the way for the local school. Sadly, the entire structure had been damaged and the entire back half of it had been ripped away. The sounds of sirens filled the eerily still air, and the flashing lights of the police cars and ambulances lit up the night sky. Coming around a corner, they saw a mass of emergency vehicles. A look of panic crossed both their faces.

When they got closer, Sarah's stomach lurched. The EMT's were wheeling two stretchers out to waiting vehicles. She didn't see faces, only the white sheets drawn up over the unfortunate persons who hadn't survived. "Oh God, Parker."

Parker managed to make it to an abandoned yard before her stomach heaved, and she emptied the contents of her stomach. Sarah rubbed her back. This was Parker's first time witnessing fatalities, and she reacted like any normal person would. Unfortunately, Sarah had seen it before. In the small town she grew up in, hunting was engrained in all the men and half the women. She remembered the first time she had seen a person hanging on to life, an errant shot finding the wrong target. When he had died, she had thrown up until there was nothing left.

Nothing can prepare a person for the shock of death, especially an unexpected death. A person didn't have the luxury of preparing himself like someone did with a person who was seriously ill, there is only a moment of shock that most people aren't emotionally or physically adept to deal with. Sarah had known that feeling, the swift sucker punch in the gut. She knew what it was to look in the eyes of a person that was leaving this world, the far off look in his eyes, the pallor of his skin, the final breath that escapes and the ultimate moment of realization of knowing that this is his last breath.

This didn't make it easier to see, only easier to deal with. It was probably worse to know the last seconds of a life cut short. She pulled Parker's body against hers, feeling sobs rack her body. After what seemed like an eternity, she felt her body still and wilt into her arms. "Come on, Cuz, let's find a place to sleep. I don't think there is anything we can do."

Chapter 4

Remy watched the news report solemnly. The damage in Oklahoma was horrible. The storm dropped five tornadoes, including the one that tore through Tushka. It was responsible for two deaths and dozens more injured. Remy sensed that Sarah had been there. She didn't know for sure, but the nagging feeling wouldn't go away. She hoped she was safe and wished she had exchanged numbers so she could have at least texted and made sure she was okay.

She and Carmen hadn't seen more than a couple small tornadoes in South Dakota. No larger ones and fortunately no fatalities. She heard the water in the bathroom stop and knew Carmen's marathon shower was over. They had spent the day chasing, and she was ready for a drink. Carmen, on the other hand, was horny, or so she said. Thanks to her little fixation with Parker, she had spent the day talking about sex and swore tonight she was getting laid. Apparently, she was making sure that she was all groomed and ready.

"Hey, Chica, where did you say we were headed tonight?"

"I didn't." Remy yelled over the hotel hair dyer, which thanks to its impressive twelve—hundred watts, had been running for the last twenty minutes in a futile attempt to dry the mop Carmen called hair. Better dryers than that had fallen victim to her thick brown locks.

Rather than try to shout over it and have to repeat herself, she waited till Carmen plopped down on the bed beside her. "You ready?"

"Yeah." Remy cut the power on the tv and dragged all five feet ten inches off the bed with a loud groan. At twenty—nine, she shouldn't feel this sore from sitting all day. Maybe, she was just tired. No, exhausted was more like it. She felt off today. Just not her normal hundred miles an hour self. She shook her head and pulled a jacket off the chair.

They headed out to the car, the cold wind whipping around them. Spring hadn't quite hit South Dakota yet, and although it had been a little warmer today, the night brought back the colder temperatures.

"So, what are you feeling?" Remy asked once they hit the road.

"Blond for an appetizer, brunette for the main course, and I'm thinking something ginger for dessert." Carmen said saucily. "And, I might even want seconds."

Remy groaned loudly. "You are such a guy."

"Oh, and you aren't?" Carmen snickered. "Chica, I seem to remember a few times when you left with more than one woman, and you were totally game for anything."

"Yeah, maybe." Remy agreed. "I'm just not feeling it tonight. I think I just want a drink and a hot bath."

"Oh, I'm sure we could find a little something for you to heat up your bath."

"Not tonight, okay." Remy was getting antsy and frustrated and she didn't have a clue why. She shouldn't have snapped at Carmen. She was just teasing, something they always did. Sex too, was something they always talked about and wanted. But tonight, she couldn't muster up enough energy to even think about looking at a woman. "Listen, I'm sorry. I didn't mean to snap. Tonight's just not a good night for me."

"It's cool, Chica." Carmen smiled. "More for me."

Remy grunted. "Good. Maybe you will forget about Parker."

"Not likely, Chica." Carmen laughed. "That's one butch I'd like to wrap my brown legs around."

"God, your mind is always in the gutter." Remy groaned loudly.

"I can't help it. I'm Latina. I think we have an extra sex chromosome."

"You have an extra something." Remy snorted. "Hey, what about that place?"

Carmen checked out the sign in front of a colorful restaurant that was obviously a Mexican restaurant. "Gaudalajara? Can't be too bad, the parking lot is packed. I could use a 'rita to get the night started off right."

It took them twenty minutes to get seated, but the smells coming from the kitchen and the entrees whizzing by them as they waited were all the encouragement they needed to stay.

When they were finally seated and had ordered margaritas and fajitas, Remy stuffed a chip loaded with house salsa into her mouth and let out an appreciative moan. "I could fill up on chips alone."

"That good, huh?" Carmen followed suit and ate several before she spoke again. "They're good, but hopefully not the best thing I'll put in my mouth tonight."

Remy rolled her eyes at her suggestive tone. Carmen thought about sex like guys thought about sex. She liked to joke that she should have been born a boy. "So, today was kind of a bust."

"Yeah, for us." Carmen agreed and sampled the margarita that the waitress had just dropped off. "But the girls did alright."

"The girls?" Remy's brow furrowed with feigned confusion. She didn't want Carmen to know that she was well aware of who the girls were, and that Sarah hadn't been far from her thoughts all day. She couldn't deny that over the years since their one night stand, she had reminisced about that night. But lately, it haunted her. She was no stranger to loving them and leaving them, so to speak, so it puzzled her that this encounter bothered her unlike the others. Maybe not bothered her so much, but stayed with her. She couldn't remember most of their names. Yet, Sarah, she couldn't make herself forget.

"Parker and Sarah." Carmen said sarcastically. "You know, the *girls* we just saw last night. Don't think I believe for a second you didn't know who I was talking about."

"No, yeah, I know." Remy stumbled over her words nervously. She and Carmen had been together long enough that there was no way she could hide her thoughts. If she didn't figure out a way to get over them or bury them, she was apt to incriminate herself pretty quickly. "Just thinking about other stuff."

"Like what?"

"Today, where we are headed next, I don't know. Just stuff."

"Okay, fine, you got other *stuff* on your mind." Carmen was quiet long enough to make a fajita and eat half of it. "But, they did good, no?"

Remy shook her head, chewing her own dinner. "Yeah, if they were in the right place. There was a line of storms that dropped five tornadoes, a couple south of Oklahoma City. I hope they are okay."

Carmen detected a hint of protectiveness in her voice, but let it slide. "Me too. Can't have anything happen to Parker before I get a piece of that."

"Oh yeah, don't want to miss that sweet piece of ass." Remy said sarcastically.

"Don't hate." Carmen scolded jokingly. "What about you? I haven't seen you interested in anyone in ages."

"I don't know." Remy drained her margarita and signaled for another one. She toyed with the straw wrapper on the table. "You ever think about quitting?"

"Quitting what? Being a lesbian?" Carmen wrinkled her nose. "No, and I never will."

Remy laughed. "No worries on that count. Everything's fine in that department. I just mean this. Chasing, tornadoes, women. Maybe finding something to give us a little more happiness instead."

"Okay, now I'm worried." Carmen set her fork down and fixed her gaze on Remy. "What's going on with you?"

"I'm not sure." Remy shrugged. "I've been doing the same thing for nearly ten years now and sometimes I don't feel like I have accomplished anything. It's just running from one place to the next, or one woman to the next. I'm almost thirty, and I don't have a thing to show for it. I guess I just want something tangible, something to validate my existence."

"Deep stuff, Chica." Carmen's brow furrowed. "This used to be enough. What changed?"

"Who knows? Maybe I have grown up or something. Maybe I'm just tired. I love what we do, don't get me wrong. But I just wonder sometimes if it's enough. Maybe I could be doing something more important."

"You don't think this is important?" Carmen queried. "We're out there risking our lives trying to find out what makes a tornado tick. Maybe figure out a way to predict them, and in doing so, save some lives. That's not important?"

Remy rubbed her hands over her face. "No, I know it's important. I just don't want to look back on my life one day and be disappointed that I cheated myself out of something great. Like maybe, I'm only taking half of what life has given me. What if what was good enough yesterday won't be enough tomorrow? What if there is something better out there and I'm missing it by going a hundred miles an hour all the time? Does that make sense at all?"

Carmen shook her head. "I guess I don't get it, Chica. I'm happy. I thought you were too. What you need is a hot woman in your bed to get your head back in the right place, no?"

Remy opened her mouth to answer then shut it again. Carmen was great as a partner, but as far as being deep, that only referred to how far inside a woman she could bury herself. Emotionally, she was as deep as a creek. Trying to get her to understand her feeling of restlessness was like trying to make a rich man understand poverty. "Yeah, you're right. Forget I mentioned it."

Chapter 5

Remy squinted into the bright morning sun. "What's the radar looking like?"

Carmen refreshed her web browser and shaded with screen with her hand. "It's small now, but it should give us something this afternoon."

The sign welcoming them to Mississippi flew by as they ate up the miles. Two days of driving brought them to the south, where a high risk of severe weather had been issued in the states of Missouri, Kentucky, Illinois, Arkansas, Louisiana, Mississippi, Tennessee, and Alabama. High risks warnings were rarely ever issued, and they sensed the storms brewing over the large area were sure to produce multiple tornadoes.

Carmen had chosen Mississippi. With little more scientific reasoning than throwing darts at a map, she had pushed for this area, insisting that she felt this was where they should be. "Looks like a couple small supercells are moving this way, just north of Dallas. I put 'em here in a couple of hours."

"Head towards Jackson, maybe?" Remy passed a sign indicating Jackson was still ninety miles away. "If so, I need to hurry."

"Nah." Carmen shook her head and glanced at the radar again. "I'm thinking somewhere around Silver City or Lexington will give us the most action. I'd get off on

Country Road 432 and head west towards Benton. There's not a clear shot, but that will put us close."

Remy watched the low mountains roll by. They weren't tall by any means, but they certainly obscured the view as far as tornadoes were concerned. She preferred the flat plains further northwest of Mississippi. They afforded the best opportunity for spotting storms and getting good footage, and a better opportunity to study the different facets of each storm.

As much fun as she had chasing, it wasn't all about that. There was a serious side to chasing as well. It was only in recent years that scientists and chasers had started to work together to learn as much about the damaging storms as possible, and in doing so, help protect people from the violent tornadoes.

Of course, this involved some pretty dangerous maneuvering on their parts, going as far as putting themselves in the path of large tornadoes just to drop probes or launch sensors into the rotation to read anything from wind speed to direction to velocity and send it back to computers that would calculate the data. For that reason, Remy and the few adventurous souls like her were tagged extreme meteorologists.

Carmen sighed loudly. "Hope these mountains flatten out, or we are going to have a hell of a time seeing anything. I don't want to be stuck looking the other way and some bad ass tornado come sneaking over the hill and catch us by surprise."

"No kidding, we don't need another repeat of Kansas. I felt a little like Dorothy." Remy's mind flashed back to the time they had been chasing in Kansas. Tall trees lined the roads and made spotting the storm almost impossible. On this particular day, a rare EF4 tornado had formed and by the time they saw the rain—wrapped wedge tornado barreling down on them at sixty miles an hour, they had barely made it out of its path. It was also the first time she had met Sarah Phillips.

Sarah had been one of the first field meteorologists on the scene after that tornado. She had zeroed in on Remy immediately, eager to find out firsthand what it was like to outrun a tornado. Remy, on the other hand, had zeroed in on Sarah, eager to find out firsthand what a hot meteorologist was like in bed. She had sensed her lack of experience in the romance department immediately, and it only added to her appeal. At twenty—two years old, Sarah had the wide—eyed innocence that only lasted until life hardened you and made you jaded.

It hadn't taken much to talk Sarah into bed with her. Dinner, a couple of drinks, some light—hearted banter and of course stories, somewhat embellished, about her first couple of years as a chaser. Sarah was as impressed with Remy as Remy was with herself. Years ago, she had been a cocky bastard. Not afraid of anything, and in her opinion, the best damn chaser there was. It had been hard to see the look of regret on Sarah's face the following morning, knowing that she was mostly responsible for the hard edge she now saw in her eyes.

"Stop, it's the girls." Carmen's excited shout broke through her reverie. "Ooh, a flat. Guess it's time for me to swoop in and save the day."

Remy snorted loudly. "And, break a nail."

Carmen's long, brightly painted nails were a subject of constant teasing. The only thing about her that was girly was her nails. Other than that, Carmen pretended not to be a girlie girl. "Just shut up and pull over. I need to see if Parker needs our, I mean, *your* help."

They slowed to a stop behind Sarah's hail battered Chevy. She had angled the rear of the car away from the road since it was the rear tire that was completely flat, and she didn't want to get hit by a passing car. Remy stretched her five foot ten inch frame and walked over to Sarah with a big smile on her face. Glancing upwards, Sarah shielded her eyes and returned Remy's smile. She was rewarded with an even bigger smile.

"Hi, Bonneville." Remy knelt down beside her. "Fancy running into you."

Sarah glanced at Parker and Carmen, and satisfied they were occupied with each other, handed Remy the jack. "Help me please. Evan always…" She stopped. She didn't need to say that Evan had been the one to change flats if they got them. Trying to forget her was going to be impossible if she couldn't even stop talking about her.

Remy rested a hand on her shoulder and squeezed her gently. "It's okay, you know, if you need to talk about it."

"No, right now I just need to get the tire changed so I can get back on the road."

"Okay, but I'm here if you need…"

"I said it's okay." Sarah let the jack fall to the ground with a loud clang.

Remy nodded her head towards Parker. "So, how come your sidekick isn't helping?"

"Are you kidding?" Sarah snorted. "For all her boasts of being a total dude, she couldn't change a tire if her life depended on it."

"God, I hope for Carmen's sake, she's better with her hands in other areas."

"Oh gross, that's my cousin." Sarah groaned. "I do not need to know that."

Remy chuckled softly and wedged her foot against the jack. "Yeah, I guess not." She pulled on one end and felt the tire iron give just enough that she knew the nut would come loose. "So, how was Oklahoma?"

She heard Sarah gulp. "Bad, Remy. The devastation was horrible. And two sisters…well, they didn't make it. Their trailer was destroyed. Parker hasn't gotten over that."

"I know how she feels." Remy tugged on the tire iron, loosening the second nut. "Hey, can you get that?" She flicked her eyes towards her forehead. "This heat is insane."

Sarah reached over and wiped the errant bead of sweat before it rolled into Remy's eye. She felt a flutter in her stomach and her hand stilled. Her face flushed at the momentary contact, and she struggled to put it in its place. She jerked her hand away and stared at the ground, hoping Remy hadn't heard the pounding of her heart.

"Thanks." Remy shook her head, willing the haze to clear. She hadn't heard Sarah's heart, but only because her own was beating so erratically. *Jesus, Tate. Get a freaking grip.* Willing her voice not to quiver, she steered the conversation back to Parker. "I remember my first time. You know…seeing a dead body. It was a tornado that ripped through the town I grew up in. It came through during the night and there was no time for a warning to be issued. Even if they had known it was coming, the people in the trailer park never would have heard the sirens. It trashed the entire thing. Three hundred trailers and there were thirty—five left."

"You didn't…lose anyone, did you?" Sarah voice was heavy with concern.

"No, but I might as well have." Remy undid the last nut and pulled the flat tire off. She glanced up at Carmen. "Hey Vega, why don't you make yourself useful and hand me the spare?"

Sarah waited till she had the tire mounted before she made her finish the story. "So, what happened?"

"I was an EMT at the time and one of the first responders. I'd been called to accidents before, but nothing could have prepared me for what happened that night. When I stumbled on the first body, God, I wanted to run. Get away from there as fast as I could and never look back. I was twenty years old. What the fuck did I know about death?"

Remy's raspy voice chipped away at Sarah's defenses. All the years she had just assumed Remy was an insensitive prick and to find out she was anything but insensitive tested her resolve to keep her at arm's length. She squeezed Remy's shoulder. "It's something no one should have to see."

"You're right. But I had to figure out a way to steel myself to it at least for that night. I figured out a way to shut it inside until I was in a place where I could deal with it. We ended up finding twenty—five bodies. I didn't sleep for weeks after. Just kept seeing those vacant, hollow eyes. They haunted me. That's why I decided to be a chaser. There wasn't anything I could do for those people, but maybe, just maybe, I could help in the future."

"Wow." Sarah studied Remy's face. It was a mix of sadness and determination. She knew deep inside that Remy had dedicated her life to a cause, and she would do whatever she could to help the next hundred towns. Her respect for Remy jumped monumentally in that moment. "You are a better person than I am. I think I would have buried myself in something that was so far from this, so that eventually I would struggle to even remember the details."

Remy shook her head. "This you couldn't forget, no matter how hard you tried."

Sarah thought back to the fateful day that her brother had been killed on a routine hunting trip. Remy was right, she didn't forget. She would always remember his last breaths, gasping for air and begging her to help him. She could see the brief moment of peace right before he died and the glassy, faraway look before she closed his eyes for the last time. No, there wasn't a day she didn't think about that and her heart didn't break again.

"What about you?" Remy asked as she stood up, the tire successfully changed. "Why are you here?"

"Honestly?" Sarah looked at the ground. Her reason was nowhere near as noble. "You."

Remy was momentarily stunned. "Me? What on earth did I have to do with it?"

"That first day interviewing you. Hearing you talk about chasing storms, seeing the passion in your eyes. You got inside me. After talking to you, nothing else seemed good enough anymore."

"Oh." Remy couldn't think of anything else to say. She rubbed her palms on her jeans, the awkwardness of the shared moment making her a bit uncomfortable. "You never said anything."

"What could I say?" Sarah leaned her hip against the car. "I couldn't stop thinking about what you said. I left the life I knew to follow some crazy pipe dream and here I am eight years later stopped on the side of the road having to beg for help changing my tire. Or, that just listening to you talk sparked something deep inside me, and no matter how hard I tried, I couldn't forget it. Until this yearning built inside me that I couldn't deny."

"Well, that's one way of putting it." Remy teased. "I didn't know."

"How could you? We never really talked after that…well after that night."

"I'm sorry about that, you know." Remy said sincerely. "I mean not sorry for that night, it was amazing." She stopped when she saw Sarah's eyebrows narrow slightly. "I am sorry I just disappeared after that."

Sarah sighed. "I guess I didn't give you much choice. I did kick you out of the room."

"True." Remy rubbed the back of her neck. "I should have made you sit down and talk to me."

"Don't apologize. We were young and stupid." Sarah shuffled her feet. "Listen, don't worry about it. It was a long time ago. You asked how I got started and the answer was you. I didn't mean to open up the past."

Remy noticed her tone of dismissal and she swallowed back a sudden feeling of loneliness. "Yeah, okay. Listen we should go." She turned and furrowed her eyebrows. Carmen was so close to Parker it looked like they were about to lock lips. "Seriously, Vega?"

Carmen jerked back, remembering they had company, her face turning bright red. "Settle, Chica. I'm just regaling Parker with stories from our glory days."

Sarah snorted loudly and Remy turned to glare at her. "Not helping."

Parker and Carmen's snickers broke into loud laughter as Remy stomped back to their car.

"Hey, Remy." Sarah shouted. "Thank you…for changing my tire."

Chapter 6

Remy's mind played the conversation over and over. Sarah's words still haunted her. *You got inside me.* Had she? Had thoughts of Remy danced inside Sarah's head all these years? Had she carried the memories of that day and maybe that night with her? Remy would probably never know. She knew Sarah well enough to know she didn't open herself up completely to people. She may share bits and pieces, divulge morsels of herself. Just enough to draw a person in, get them hooked without them even knowing then quietly sneak away without so much as a trace.

It wasn't normal for her to spend so much time obsessing over a past conquest and wasn't that all Sarah was? Someone that she had hooked up with. Remy didn't let herself get involved beyond meaningless relationships. Lately though, she was questioning everything that made up who she was. Somehow, the shallow, meaningless trysts she had grown accustomed to weren't enough anymore. Suddenly, she craved more and the thought awed her and unnerved her at the same time.

Seeing Sarah stirred up memories and feelings that she struggled to process. Remy always categorized her past encounters, but Sarah wouldn't fit in the box she had made for her. Her tidy world was veering off course and it unsettled her. She couldn't remember a time she had ever been so confused. She glanced over at Carmen who was still wearing a goofy—ass grin and rolled her eyes. Not the person she could talk this through with. That left her alone with her thoughts and figuring out why all of a sudden someone mattered.

"Know what Parker told me?" Carmen's voice broke into her thoughts.

"Huh? No, what?"

"She says that apparently Sarah is different lately. Pre—occupied somehow." There was a suggestive tone to Carmen's voice as if she were telling Remy something she should have already known.

"So?"

"So, Parker thinks it's you."

Remy's stomach twisted in knots. She could pretend she didn't know what Carmen meant, but she would only be fooling herself. Still, she couldn't share her private thoughts with Carmen, so she played dumb. "Me, what?"

"Parker thinks that you and Sarah had something in the past, and Sarah hasn't been able to let it go."

Remy choked. "That's the craziest thing I've ever heard."

"Is it?"

Carmen's gaze burned into Remy's profile till she could stand it no longer.

"What?" Remy said with exasperation.

"I think it makes total sense." Carmen opined. "Parker says that Sarah is different lately and especially when you're around."

"Oh and Parker is the expert on people now?"

"I'm not saying that." Carmen said defensively. "But, they are cousins, and she spends every day with Sarah. So, she would have a pretty good idea of what's up. Plus, there is you."

Remy looked at her askance. "There is me, what?"

"Well, you are different too. More serious. Introspective. And, you're nice to Sarah."

"I'm nice to everyone."

"Not exactly, Chica. I've seen you in action with women for years now. With any other one, all you care about is getting them into bed. You don't give a rat's ass about her feelings. But Sarah, she's different. You care."

Remy threw up her hands. "I thought we were supposed to be chasing today, not deconstructing my behavior."

"Whoa there, Tate." Carmen's tone was serious and Remy knew she was in trouble. When Carmen called her Tate, it was usually followed by a lecture.

"Listen, I'm sorry. I didn't mean to snap." She rubbed her eyes. "I'm just tired and worn out. It's not you, okay?"

"But, maybe it is me." Serious Carmen was out and on the prowl now. "Maybe I hit the nail on the head and it bothers you that you finally met someone you care about. *Ms. Untouchable Bad Ass Tate* isn't as heartless and detached as she wants us to think she is. You're human, you're an emotional creature just like the rest of the world."

"That's not it at all. Tell Parker to sell her romance theory elsewhere. I've been around Sarah too. She isn't any more interested in me than I am in her."

Her words might as well have fallen on deaf ears. For all her bravado, she didn't believe them anymore than Carmen did. Her loud snort was enough to let Remy know that her words of protestation meant nothing.

"So, can we get back to the storm?" Remy nodded out the windshield at the darkening sky. "Let's not forget why we're here."

"Oh, I haven't forgotten. I can't, not with you beside me. I've known you a long time and this is the job. You live the job. You are so focused all the time on this that you miss what's going on around you. I guess it's nice to finally see you showing some emotion."

"I'm not show…" Remy clapped her mouth shut. "Do you mean that? You think I'm all about the job and nothing else?"

"Yeah, I do. Don't get me wrong. That's good, especially out here. You have to focus because we get in life or death situations, but off the clock, you don't let loose. You're untouchable. If you stopped giving me a hard time, you would see that I actually really like Parker."

"You do?" Remy studied Carmen's face, trying to gauge her feelings. "You really like her, huh?"

"All you see is the player looking to score. This time, I think it could be serious." Carmen confessed. "She's different, Rem. I can't quite put my finger on it. Don't get me wrong, I want to do the horizontal mambo with her for sure, but this time I'd kind of like her to stick around after."

"Wow." Remy ran a hand through her messy hair. "I didn't realize. I mean, you just met and all."

"I know, it's crazy. But there's something there with this one, and I'm going to explore where it goes." Carmen blushed, which was almost imperceptible under her brown skin. "This girl may finally be ready to settle down."

"I'm speechless." Remy made several noises to herself. "I did not see that coming. The hot—blooded Latina, who set out to sleep with as many American women as possible, is looking to play house with just one girl."

"I can hardly believe it myself." Carmen chuckled. "I guess I just found the right Gringo."

Remy chuckled more to herself than at Carmen's comment. She'd known Carmen more years than she could count and no one, no matter how wonderful they had been, had gotten to her. Parker must be different. It shouldn't have surprised her. Sarah was becoming more special than Remy would have ever imagined, so why wouldn't her cousin be the same? They were cut from the same cloth.

"Mierda!" Carmen shouted in her family's native Spanish. Remy followed her finger and saw the large mesocyclone looming in front of them. Shit was quite appropriate, although the closer they drove she thought holy fuck might work just as well. She slowed considerably, eyeing the massive storm. She could see quickening rotation in the wall cloud and knew it would probably be dropping a tornado any minute now.

Remy thought about the small town they had just passed and given the storm's current direction, she knew it stood right in the path of a potentially horrific storm. She picked up her cell and dialed quickly. When the tinny voice answered on the other end, she identified herself and let them know that the supercell heading towards the town looked like it was going to drop at least one twister right over the town. "Shit, shit. Change that, funnel spotted." She checked the mile marker and shouted over the increasing din of the wind. "Tornado down, twelve miles southwest of Yazoo City."

She pulled over, parked the car and grabbed her video camera. "Vega, camera. Let's go!" Her words were pointless. Carmen was out of the car almost before it stopped. She set up a tripod and pointed the camera towards the massive tornado, now over a quarter of a mile wide. "Oh shit, Rem. She's huge!"

Remy barely heard her over the roar barreling down on them. She thought she had pulled far enough out of the way, but the tornado had shifted and was coming straight towards them and fast.

"We gotta go! We gotta move!" Carmen was already in, but Remy stood there, tucked behind the car to block the dust and debris that was blowing directly towards her at over eighty miles an hour. She didn't want to move, she needed to see the massive storm up close, feel its maddening, reckless fury.

"Come on, Rem! Shit, don't be stupid." Carmen shouted over the wind, and her words were carried away seemingly unheard. Her pulse was beating erratically. The twister was close, too close, and Remy wasn't budging.

The first drops of rain splattered randomly on the windshield and soon, tiny bits of ice pinged on the hood. Remy pulled her hood over her head and put her hand over the camera to protect the lens. She couldn't move, didn't want to move. Somehow the storm was a part of her, every tumultuous, haphazard rotation mirrored her life. Unsettled at every turn, chaos instead of order.

A tennis ball sized chunk of hail hit the hood near her and the impact finally woke her up. She looked through the windshield and saw the frightened eyes of her partner and knew she'd gone too far. She straightened up and a strong gust of wind blew her off her feet, upending her in a shallow, water filled ditch. "Fuck!" The water soaked her clothes immediately, and as she struggled to right herself, the closeness of the tornado caught her off guard. She grabbed the camera, which, miraculously, had fallen clear of the water, and locked herself in the safety of the truck. "I'm sorry."

"You can apologize later, Chica. Just get me the fuck out of here!" Carmen shouted.

Remy maneuvered the truck in a tight u—turn and gunned the engine. The tires slipped on the wet, debris—filled road, so she let off the engine, allowing the tires to take hold then put the pedal to the floor. She watched the now half—mile wide wedge out the passenger window and prayed the people of Yazoo City had been warned. The truck had a hemi, but with thousands of pounds of steel attached to it, the engine struggled to generate the speed needed to outrun the storm. Her next words came in a whisper. "Oh shit."

The edges of the tornado had overtaken them. Her only choice was to keep going and pray Thor's weight kept them on the ground.

Carmen's eyes were closed and her hands were clasped so tightly, they were completely white. Her lips moved in a silent prayer.

Remy had to keep both hands on the wheel, and she hoped the small camera mounted on the top of the truck was recording the storm. She knew the sensors were working.

She could hear the steady beeps coming from the recorder behind her and knew that it was busy cataloguing wind speed, velocity, direction. All measurements that were vital in hopefully one day knowing enough about tornadoes that there would no longer be loss of life associated with these horrific storms.

She grabbed glimpses of the tornado, thankfully growing smaller in the side mirror. Pulling to a safe distance, south of the storm's track, she stopped once more. This time she stayed in the truck and filmed from the safety inside. "Oh shit, it's getting the power lines. Oh God, a house, it's got a house. Please let there be no one home." She watched in horror as the tornado picked up the large farmhouse and tossed it aside like grains of sand.

She could see the small town of Yazoo City in the direct line of the twister, and she put her hand over her mouth and tried to push the rising bile back down. The skies were littered with what she recognized as pieces of houses, whole trees thrashed about like playthings. A town's hopes and dreams ripped away by a faceless killer.

No matter how many times she witnessed this, it never got any easier. Nothing could make this part less hard to watch. Every time they found out that there were victims, another little part of her died. Another part of her felt like a failure. Wasn't her whole point in being a chaser to help people live? And yet, they continued to experience loss of life with every new season.

She never seriously thought about giving up. She didn't answer her failures with defeat, but with a renewed sense of determination. Quitting wasn't an option, at least not one that she would ever allow herself. There was too much at stake, too many lives to be saved, and she still believed that with enough chases, with enough data, that one day, she might make a difference. Her stubbornness made her indefatigable.

She finally looked at Carmen who was still pale. "I'm sorry. I should never have gotten us that close."

Carmen turned, anger burning in her eyes. "What the fuck, tonta?"

Remy winced. It had been a long time since Carmen had been this mad and there was nothing she could say or do to fix it. "Carmen, come on, we got out…"

Carmen cut her off. She got out of the truck and slammed the door hard enough to shake Thor, which was not easy to do.

Remy swallowed guiltily and got out, running after Carmen, grabbing her arm and trying to stop her.

"Get away from me." Carmen seethed angrily. She was more frightened than she had ever been. She broke Remy's grasp and stalked away.

Remy jogged after her. "Come on, C. You know I would never do anything to hurt you."

"Vete a la mierda!" Carmen started walking the other way, shouting at Remy. She only caught half of it. In her anger, half the words were in Spanish, so Remy could only imagine what she was being called.

"Tu es pendeja!"

"Tú me estás jodiendo."

Remy watched her pace, catching enough to know that it would be awhile before she calmed down.

Hours later, as they drove through the small town, the devastation overwhelmed her. They had talked to the local sheriff and the unofficial death toll was ten. Her heart broke again. It was on days like these that she felt immensely guilty that she had pulled Carmen into her quest. It was on days like these that a small part of her wanted to run away and forget the horrors she had seen. It was also on days like these, that faces from her past haunted her, and voices whispered in her ears. And, she couldn't say no to their pleas.

Chapter 7

Sarah ran her hands over her face. The dark circles under her eyes gave away the stress she'd been trying to hide. Even a hot shower had done little to wash away her tiredness. She had even refused Parker's invitation for dinner, choosing to spend a few hours alone in their hotel room. Today's chase had been especially difficult on them. Ten more people had died in the storm that dropped eighty—eight tornadoes by the time it was said and done.

The wedge that devastated Yazoo City was a massive mile and a half wide EF4 tornado. The winds had reached 150 miles an hour. The town didn't stand a chance, and the few people that had not managed to get to safety, had given their lives as the ultimate sacrifice. She shook her head, sad at the unneeded loss of life.

A knock on the door startled her then she laughed at herself. Parker was back and had obviously lost her room key, which didn't surprise her. She pulled the chain off, which she had secured only because she was by herself and in the shower. When she opened the door, she couldn't keep the surprise off her face. "Hi."

"Hi." Remy smiled sheepishly. "Wanna beer?"

Sarah stood back and Remy walked past her, depositing the six—pack on the small hotel table. She looked around the room, which looked a lot like hers, bland and depressing.

She met Sarah's inquisitive gaze and smiled wryly. "My room's a bit occupied at the moment."

Sarah's mind flashed briefly to Parker and knew without Remy saying anything that she and Carmen must have kicked her out of the room. "Ahh, gotcha, it seemed like she had been gone a while."

"I, uhh, didn't think they would have liked an audience. Do you mind if I hang here a while?"

Sarah shook her head side—to—side. "That's fine." She was suddenly on edge. Remy's sudden appearance got her mind off the day, but it put her senses in overdrive. She didn't want to like her as much as she did. Remy already preoccupied her thoughts more than she cared to admit and she tried to ignore the intimacy of the two of them alone in her room. She pulled her robe tighter against her body. "I'm just going to put some clothes on."

"Don't do it on my account." Remy offered. She opened a beer and handed it to Sarah as she passed. "You look comfortable."

"I would just feel better if I wasn't so under—dressed."

Remy put a hand on Sarah's arm, stopping her. Her gaze met Sarah's and held it, her eyes searching Sarah's face. Finally, she found the answer. "I'm not going to try anything."

"It's not that, I'm cold." Sarah stammered quickly. She should have been surprised that Remy could read her thoughts, but she wasn't. It had always been that way. Somehow, Remy could look deep inside her soul and know what she was thinking. It unnerved her, Remy unnerved her. She got to her in a way that even Evan had not been able to. "I'll be right back." She took the beer and almost ran to the bathroom, leaving Remy wondering where the fire was.

Remy took another beer, screwed off the top and took a long swig. Her stomach rumbled loudly. Funny, two minutes ago she couldn't even think about eating. Now, an unexplained calmness flowed through her veins. She could have tried to attribute it to the alcohol, but one drink wasn't enough to do anything. No, she knew what had settled her down. Sarah. Just seeing her was enough to calm her frayed nerves. She couldn't put her finger on it. It was just a sense of peace that overtook her and reined in her runaway thoughts when she was in Sarah's presence. "Hey, did you eat? Are you hungry?"

Sarah's heart skipped a beat at the sound of Remy's voice. Somewhere between a one night stand and tonight, they had slipped into this friendliness that surprised her. She was no longer angry at Remy for what she had once thought of as taking advantage of her. She could now accept it for what it was. Lust at first sight that had led to a night of the most amazing sex she could remember. And now, it was as if they had very easily become good friends. She cracked open the door. "Yeah, getting there."

"What do you feel like?" Remy walked towards the open door, taking it as her invitation to talk at the door. She pushed it open and her breath caught. Sarah was pulling a shirt over her head and her breasts were bare. Her eyes took in every inch of her smooth, creamy skin. Her brown nipples stood out from Sarah's body. She pictured her mouth on those nipples and her knees buckled slightly. She wanted to stare, but the threat of getting caught gaping like a randy little boy made her back pedal quickly.

Her heart was beating erratically and when Sarah came out of the bathroom, she must have noticed the slight flush in her face. "You okay?"

"No. Yes. I'm fine." Remy held her beer up as if explaining her red face. "Beer face."

Sarah's brow furrowed. "Ooo—kay. What were you hungry for?"

Remy shrugged. "I was thinking Chinese. Takeout okay? I'm not feeling like going out anywhere tonight."

Sarah knew she had read her mind again. "That's perfect."

Remy grabbed a phone book out of the drawer and flipped through the pages till she found one that was close. She dialed and waited for someone to answer. Surprisingly, the voice on the other end spoke almost perfect English with just a hint of an accent. She hadn't asked Sarah what she preferred, and she could see by her narrowed eyes that it had not gone unnoticed. "Delivery. We need an order of Hunan beef, orange chicken, shrimp Lo Mein, two orders of crab Rangoon, and four egg rolls. Umm, one brown rice, one white."

Sarah watched her shut her phone and shot her a look. "Which one of those is for me?"

Remy at least had the courtesy to blush. "Sorry, I'm bad about that. I should have asked."

"Yeah, you should have." Sarah chided. "You're lucky though, I like two out of three of those. You can have the Lo Mein all to yourself."

Remy laughed, relief evident in her features. "But, the rest was okay?"

"Yes. The rest was perfect." She sat on the bed across from Remy. "This place any good?"

"I don't know. Never been there. I'll let you know once I taste the Rangoon." She caught Sarah's questioning look. "You can tell how good a place is by their crab Rangoon."

"Has any one ever told you what a weirdo you are?" Sarah teased.

"Maybe once or twice." Remy toyed with the label on her bottle. "Normally, it's Carmen."

"Oh yeah, speaking of Carmen, what happened tonight?"

Remy gave a short laugh. "Not sure, exactly. One minute we are getting ready to go someplace to get a drink and the next thing I know, Parker shows up at the door. Apparently, she and Carmen had cooked up this plan to meet up. I sort of got kicked out of the room."

"Sounds like Parker." Sarah settled back against the headboard. "She's kind of a player. I hope Carmen knows that."

"Me too." Remy confessed. "She's too old for me to tell her what to do, but I hope she's careful. She really likes Parker and I'm hoping that the feeling's mutual or that Parker lets her down easy. I've never seen Carmen so…what's the word I'm looking for? Enamored."

"Oh." Sarah's brow furrowed. "I'm not sure Parker is into the serious thing."

Remy shrugged her shoulders. "Oh well, they're both adults. Although, I may have to punch Parker if she hurts Carmen at all."

Sarah laughed out loud. "I may have to hold her while you do it."

A loud knock on the door made them both jump. "Damn, that is the fastest take out I've ever seen."

"Or, Parker has lost her touch." Sarah teased. She watched Remy amble towards the door, her lean body filling her jeans out nicely. Her bottom was deliciously round and toned. Sarah pictured her hands cupping her bottom, pulling her tight to her body as Remy pounded into her, stroking them both to a climax. She felt heat rising into her cheeks and looked down quickly when Remy brought her a carton of food.

It would do her no good to get worked up over Remy again. No matter how attracted she was to her or how amazing the sex had been, she wasn't letting herself reopen that door. She was older now, older and wiser. Sleeping with Remy was her past, not her now. She would take friendship and offer the like, but no more.

Remy set the rest of the food on the nightstand between the two beds. She fiddled with her food and watched the emotions play across Sarah's face. Whatever she was wrestling with, she must have reached a conclusion. She watched her jaw set with determination. Were they any closer, she would have tried to pry the information out of her. As it was, she didn't think she needed to ask. She sensed it had something to do with her. Oddly, she was struck by the resolution in Sarah's eyes and she felt suddenly empty.

"Thank you." Sarah had torn into her orange chicken, her hunger reawakened by the delicious smells now filling the room.

"You're welcome." Remy sat silently for several moments, content to just enjoy Sarah's company. Finally full, she set the empty carton beside her and sighed loudly. "I ate way too much."

"God, me too." Sarah agreed, glad she had put on jogging pants and not her tighter jeans. At the time, she had done it to look as unappealing to Remy as possible, and now, she congratulated her foresight.

Remy watched her and she felt warmth effuse her body. Sarah was beautiful. Her shoulder length brown hair was wavy tonight, obviously towel dried from the shower and not blown out. She liked it that way. Her eyes seemed happier now, not as dark as they had some weeks before. Remy had thought her attractive before, but now she was beautiful. "Can I ask you a personal question?"

Sarah's eyes narrowed almost imperceptibly and she crossed her arms over her chest. To a casual observer, it would have meant nothing, but to Remy, it spoke volumes. It let her know that they may be forming a tentative friendship, but Sarah's personal life was going to stay her personal life. "That depends."

"On what?" Remy leaned forward. The door on Sarah's life wasn't locked, maybe just closed.

"On the question." Sarah paused to take a drink. When she leaned over to put the bottle back on the nightstand, Remy could see the curve of her breasts and her pulse jumped. Being this close had its advantages, but also put her at a disadvantage. Normally, if she were attracted to someone and they were holed up in a hotel room on a rainy night, she wouldn't be talking. She pulled her eyes away, but not before Sarah caught her staring.

Remy had the decency to at least blush. She almost thought better of the question she wanted to ask, the answer haunting her more recently than she dared admit. "Do you ever think about that night?"

If the question threw Sarah at all, she did a great job of hiding her reaction. She could have pretended that she had no clue what Remy was talking about, but one glance in her eyes and Sarah knew and could almost feel her caress anew. "Really, don't hold back."

Remy smiled sheepishly. "Sorry. My mouth, it always gets me in trouble."

"If I remember correctly, it got you in trouble several times that night."

"Ahh, so you do remember." Remy smiled, not the cocky smile she normally used, but a sweet, almost shy smile. It pleased her to no end to know that that night hadn't been forgotten.

"Yeah, I do. Actually, the first few months, I thought about it all the time. I was mortified that I jumped into bed with a total stranger and did things I had only heard of before. I can't say I'm very proud of myself. Now when I think about it, it's more in a life lesson kind of way." Sarah watched the emotions on Remy's face, and she felt guilty at the hurt that was there, because of her. But she was resolute. She made those mistakes when she was younger, well one mistake really, since it was a one—time thing. Now, she wouldn't dream of jumping in the sack with someone she had just met. She wasn't a prude, just not a woman that slept with someone just because she could. "Don't get me wrong. I'll admit, and only to this one thing, it was amazing. You were amazing. But, that was a different me."

Remy studied her face closely. She wanted to break that stone exterior, get back inside Sarah. Somehow, she needed to do that to define their relationship, to put it in some neat compartment and tuck it away. "How about now? We know each other pretty well. Eight years is a long time to get to know someone. I figure we are long overdue for our next hookup."

Sarah choked on her beer and nearly sprayed it all over the room. "Are you serious? Why does everything have to be about sex with you? Can't you just have a friend you aren't trying to coax into bed?"

Remy shrugged. "That's what Carmen is for. We haven't ever slept together, and I can honestly say I have no desire to. I guess it's different with you. I'm attracted to you, more now than I was before, and that was enough to stick with me all this time. I like our friendship, but to put it bluntly, I want to sleep with you."

This time the beer did go all over the room. The wide—eyed look in Sarah's face would have been almost comical if Remy had been joking. But she was dead serious. She just needed to figure out a way to make Sarah see that.

"I'm not interested in a one night stand with you." Sarah said defensively.

"How about more than one night?" Remy teased.

Sarah shook her head, got up and headed into the bathroom. She came out with a towel and started to dry herself off. "The Remy I know doesn't do relationships."

"And you don't think I can change?" Remy countered and caught the towel as it came flying towards her. She hadn't gotten too wet but enough that she accepted it with a thank you. "It's been a long time Sarah, people change." Remy held her gaze, needing her to believe.

"Not you, Remy. I've known you a long time and it's always the same." Sarah sat back down facing her. "People change, I've changed. It's a nice notion. I just don't get the Remy buying into the whole settle down with one person bit."

"Maybe, I just hadn't met the right person yet."

"I'm not special, Remy." Sarah leaned forward and forced Remy to look her in the eyes. "And, don't think for a second that I'm falling for your whole maybe you're the one bit. I'm not as naïve as I used to be."

Remy rubbed her hands on her jeans, sensing this was the end of the conversation for now. "Fair enough. You're probably right anyway. People like me don't change."

Sarah heard the catch in her voice and immediately regretted her harsh words. "I didn't mean that, I'm sure you can change. I just meant I'm nothing special."

"Sarah, it's okay. You're right about one thing. I'm a cad. I always have been and I guess I always will be." Remy stood up and walked towards the door. "But, you're wrong about one thing, Sarah. You are special, whether you choose to believe that or not. Thanks for letting me hang out here and for the company. I enjoyed it. At the very least, I think there's a chance we can be pretty good friends."

Sarah watched Remy leave too quickly for her to respond. She did like Remy, but there was no way she could open that door again. It had taken too long to get over her the first time. Right now, with Evan leaving her for another woman, she didn't think she could stand to be hurt again.

Chapter 8

"So, rough night last night?" Sarah teased.

Parker groaned and let her head rest against the seat. "I have never been twisted in so many positions by anyone. Holy hell, they weren't joking when they said Latin lovers were the best."

"That good, huh?" Sarah chuckled.

"Oh my fucking God. I can honestly say that parts of me hurt so good this morning." Parker pulled her sunglasses up and regarded Sarah thoughtfully. "What about you? Get into anything fun last night?"

Sarah colored slightly. "Umm, no. I had dinner, drank a beer and fell asleep watching tv."

"By yourself?" Parker's tone suggested she knew something she wasn't saying out loud.

"Of course. Who would I be hanging out with?"

"Oh, no one. Remy might have mentioned that she was going to run by after we kicked her out." Parker cocked an eyebrow and smiled like the Cheshire cat.

"Okay, fine. Yes, Remy came by. We had dinner and chatted." Sarah's voice went up an octave, a sign that she was not being completely truthful.

"Hmm. Sounds fun. TV, huh?"

"Yes, dinner and TV." She glared at Parker. "That's it, nothing happened."

"If you say so."

"So, tell me about last night, besides the pretzel sex."

Parker laughed out loud. "Okay, sex aside. She could be the one."

"Kind of early to make that determination, don't you think?"

"Mmm, maybe, if I were you. But, since I don't have to analyze pages and pages of statistical data to ascertain if we are a mathematical match, and I can just go with my gut, I can honestly tell you that I knew the first time I saw her."

Parker dodged the empty cup Sarah threw at her. "Sorry, hun, it's true. You over think everything. Tell me one time in your life you did something without thinking."

"Remy." Sarah threw her name out without thinking and instantly wished she could retract the rash comment.

"What?!"

"I mean this. I became a storm chaser right after the first time I ran into Remy." Sarah stammered, trying to explain something completely different than what she meant. There was a time she had jumped without a second thought. Look where it had gotten her. Completely naked with a woman she had just met. But, God, she had wanted Remy, and damn it if she wasn't feeling the same way lately, much to her chagrin.

"Uh—huh." Parker's tone implied she didn't believe that explanation for one second. "You're sure that's it? Doesn't seem so crazy. It's a job. People jump careers all the time. And you did want to be a meteorologist anyway, so this isn't really all that different, just more extreme. I still stand by the fact that you don't do anything without analyzing it to death."

Sarah sighed. "I will admit I am that way in a lot of things. But, I can be spontaneous too."

"Oh yeah?" Parker cocked an eyebrow. "So, be spontaneous. Do something crazy."

"Okay, fine, I will."

"Do something crazy…like sleep with Remy." Parker quipped.

"That's not crazy. That's just stupid. I'm not even attracted to her." Sarah's hands tightened on the wheel and her heart jumped into her throat. "Besides, I'm just not a one night stand kind of girl."

The second the words left her mouth, she wished them back. Once, she had been that kind of girl. She couldn't help it though. She wanted Remy, and she had wanted her bad. The woman was a walking orgasm. Tall and lanky, with long, fluid muscles. Her piercing green eyes had looked deep inside Sarah's soul and turned her completely inside out. The lock of unruly sandy blond hair hung perpetually in her face, and Sarah had wanted to brush it out of her eyes the moment they had met. She hadn't just been attracted to her, Sarah had been head over heels in lust with her, and she couldn't have behaved that night even if she tried.

"That's funny. The blush on your face tells me otherwise." Parker teased. "I know she's attracted to you. You can see it in her eyes and the way her body talks to you. It's like her skin is longing to feel your body against it."

"That's crazy." Sarah protested with a wave of her hand. She knew it was just as it had been all those years ago. "You can't get that from seeing us together a couple of times."

"Can't I?" Parker's tone was suddenly serious. "She is easy to read. More so than you and we are related. I know she's interested, whether you want to believe it or not. So, again, I say do something spontaneous. I'm not asking you to make a commitment. God knows I wouldn't do that, not after the whole fiasco with Evan. But, for God sake, have some fun for once in your life."

You mean twice in my life, don't you? Sarah's mind flashed to Remy's naked body pressed tightly against her. She had given herself completely that night, a wanton woman. And, she had loved every minute of it. Remy's tongue had elicited wave after wave of intense pleasure and left Sarah longing for more.

She had lied to Remy earlier. She thought about that night all the time. And her traitorous body still reacted to her touch after all these years. She shouldn't have, but she had to admit there were times when she had been with Evan that she imagined Remy instead just to come. Maybe that was one of the reasons things had never been perfect with them. She couldn't give herself completely when so much of her mind was still occupied with thoughts of someone else.

"Let's just drop it for now, okay?" Sarah pleaded. "Maybe, I'll surprise you one day."

"Maybe." Parker said cryptically. She had watched Sarah's face and the myriad of emotions that flashed across it. She knew as much as Sarah protested, there was a part of her that was attracted to Remy, and maybe open to doing just what Parker had dared her to do. Maybe, just maybe, Parker would be around to see it.

"So, anyway, back to you." Sarah suggested. "Tell me about Carmen and why she's the one. I mean might be the one."

"She reminds me of Mom."

Sarah crinkled her brow. "Your mom? She's about as Irish as they come. Carmen is Puerto Rican. How on earth could she remind you of your mom?"

"Mmm, true. All that aside, she's one of the sweetest people I know." Parker's face lit up in a goofy grin. "Do you know she asked me if she could kiss me last night? And, she said please. Nobody's ever asked me if they could kiss me. They just assume because I'm a butch that I'm supposed to do the asking. Or, I'm just supposed to take the lead. It's sexy as all get out when a beautiful woman takes charge."

"Okay, polite, that's one thing. Although, I'm not sure you can build a relationship on just a please here and there."

Parker rolled her eyes. "Uhh, hello, don't you think I know that? Not only is she sweet, she has a great sense of humor. I've laughed more with her than I have in forever."

"Hey, I'm funny."

"Looking." Parker snorted. "Family is really important to her. And, she is insanely attractive. She makes my knees weak just looking at her. Then there's this thing she does with her…"

Sarah stuck her fingers in her ears. "La, la, la, I don't want to hear this."

Parker burst out laughing. "Fine, Cuz. I'll spare you the details. I just know she makes me feel more special than anyone ever has."

"Well, I guess that's got to count for something." Sarah conceded. "So, I'm guessing you have their itinerary for the next couple of days."

Parker's face turned red. "Maybe."

"Which way are they headed?"

"Back up to Kansas. Remy said there was a cold front moving in from Canada, and it was going to run into a warm front that was headed up the Gulf. Figured there would be pretty good storms up that way." Parker pulled up the radar and scanned the Midwest. "Nothing right now except a few smaller rainstorms moving through Michigan. It's totally clear here."

Here was just south of Little Rock, Arkansas. They had gotten a late start. Partly due to Sarah not moving around very well this morning. After Remy left the night before, Sarah had finished off the six—pack she left. That meant she had five beers, three more than normal, and she was feeling the residual effects. Advil and lots of coffee had helped, but Parker's incessant giddiness was difficult to stomach.

They had only been on the road for three hours, and she was already tired of driving. "Do you mind driving?"

Parker's eyes nearly bugged out of her head. "Drive? Me? Have you lost your mind?" Sarah didn't let her drive. At least she hadn't up to that point. Curiosity almost pushed her to ask why the sudden change, but she could see from the crease in her cousin's brow that she was obviously not up to par.

"Maybe. I don't know that I can trust Chevy to your unskilled driving." Sarah teased.

"You okay?" Parker was suddenly serious.

"Yeah, I'm fine. Just a little headache. I just need to close my eyes for a while." Sarah pulled the car over and turned on the flashers as she slowed to a stop. "You don't mind, do you?"

Parker shook her head. "Mind? Are you kidding? I've already changed my status on facebook. *Finally driving Ms. Daisy.*"

Sarah laughed and got out when there was a break in traffic. "Just shut up and drive."

Parker got in and immediately pulled the seat up. She was a good four inches shorter than Sarah, and her feet barely reached the pedals. She eased her way back onto the road and joined the steady flow of traffic on I—40. It turned into an interstate just a few miles outside of Little Rock, and she was glad to leave the two—lane road and the slower speeds behind.

Like her life, which she lived on fast and faster, her lead foot had her riding in the passing lane for most of the trip. She wasn't sure where they were heading yet, and rather than bother Sarah, who had already nodded off, she kept driving west on 40. Two hours later, they pulled into a travel stop just outside Oklahoma City. Her bladder was screaming at her, and she needed a Mt. Dew badly.

Though she had tried to ease into a spot and stop without waking Sarah, when she shut off the engine, Sarah's eyes popped open. "Where are we?"

"Just outside Oklahoma City."

"Oh wow, you should have woken me up. I didn't mean to sleep the whole time."

"It's cool, you looked like you could use a little power nap."

Sarah rubbed her eyes tiredly. "Yeah, maybe so."

Parker opened her door and started to get out. "You want anything?"

"Oddly enough, an Icee."

"Okay, who are you and what have you done with my cousin?" Parker teased. "An Icee? We haven't had those since we were kids and snuck out of daycare at the church and ran to the Seven—Eleven."

"I don't know. Crazy, huh?"

Parker walked into the gas station shaking her head. She walked up and down the aisles till she found a King Size Snickers, a bag of Nacho Combos and a Mt. Dew. She hadn't seen an Icee machine and wasn't sure what to get instead. She settled on a fountain Cherry Coke.

When she handed the drink to Sarah, she shot her an apologetic smile. "Sorry, no Icee. Cherry Coke okay? If not, I'll run back in and grab you something else."

Sarah took a long swig of her drink, surprised to discover it quenched her thirst quite well. It was cherry after all. "No, this is good. Thank you."

Parker held the Combos out to Sarah, but she only shook her head no. "Snickers?"

"No, thanks. I'm not really hungry." She took another drink and lay back against the headrest. "You know I'm not feeling Kansas. Something's brewing here. I pulled up the radar. There's a small string of storms a couple of hours west of here and there's already some rotation in the cells. Let's head a little south of the city."

Parker nodded quietly. She knew they would miss Carmen, and although she had only left her hours before, she already missed her.

Sarah was fighting her own inner struggle. Her mind wanted to give in and follow Remy to Kansas, but her gut told her to stay put. No matter what her feelings were regarding Remy, and honestly, she hadn't been able to put a name to them, this took first place. She felt safe knowing that Remy would have made the same decision. Or, at least, she thought she would. After all, Remy was here because she honestly believed she could help people.

Parker navigated through the late afternoon traffic around Oklahoma City with ease. As much as Sarah liked to keep hold of the reins, Parker had always been comfortable behind the wheel. She'd been driving since she was knee high to a grasshopper, as her Grandmother had once said. Growing up in a small farm town meant pitching in with family chores, and that included driving the family tractor from very early on.

They hadn't spoken since the gas station. Sarah wasn't sure if it was just because she was tired or if Parker was upset with her for choosing to stay here. "I'm sorry, Parker."

"It's okay." Parker winked. "There are plenty of places to stop between here and there." She turned south on 35 and watched Sarah's face, waiting for her to signal when to stop.

"This is good." Sarah pointed at the sign for Norman. "Pull over here and get comfy. We're gonna be waiting a while."

Parker shut off the engine and reclined the seat. She pulled her ball cap over her eyes and yawned loudly. "Wake me up when the show starts."

Sarah chuckled softly. Parker could fall asleep anywhere, and in the same time it took a puppy to fall asleep. All she had to do was close her eyes and she was out.

Sarah pulled her Kindle out of the glove box and powered it up. She was knee deep in Gerri Hill's latest thriller set out west. Several minutes into the book, the story line of the two heroines fighting their mounting attraction had her mind wandering to Remy. It didn't matter that she tried hard to forget her, and the more she tried, the more she thought about Remy.

"How long have you been doing this?" Remy leaned in and Sarah caught her breath. Up close, her green eyes were even more alluring.

"Not…not long." Sarah managed to stutter. The breeze was carrying Remy's scent into her nostrils, and she forced herself not to lean closer. She smelled of summer and rain and sex. Sarah wasn't completely naïve, but nothing could have prepared her for the way Remy had her heart racing. She tried to back up, but her knees hit the bed, and she started to fall backwards.

Before she could blink, Remy's arm wrapped around her back, and she pulled her body tightly against hers. "You have the most beautiful blue eyes I've ever seen."

Sarah swallowed a lump in her throat. "I bet you say that to all the girls."

Remy shook her head from side—to—side. "No, only you." If it were possible, Remy pulled her body even closer. Her hazel eyes were dark green with desire. Her gaze dropped to Sarah's lips, and she leaned in closer.

Sarah waited for the alarms to go off in her head, but they didn't. The only sound she heard was her own shallow breathing and her heart beating rapidly in her chest. She licked her lips subconsciously, and Remy took that as her cue. She pressed her lips against Sarah's softly, caressing them until Sarah's lips opened and allowed her entry.

Remy ran her tongue along Sarah's lower lip and she felt her quiver in her arms. She smiled to herself, amazed at how easy it was to kiss this woman she had only known a few hours. When their tongues met for the first time, she felt her own heart hammering inside her chest. She deepened the kiss as her hands started to roam over Sarah's back lightly.

Sarah's body leaned into Remy's, aching to feel her naked skin pressed against hers. She ran her hands under Remy's shirt and swallowed the moan that escaped her lips. The need for Remy's touch was growing within her, and she needed to quench it. Not normally one to be the aggressor, Sarah felt her body take over. She ran her hands over Remy's stomach and over her small, perfect breast. She wasn't surprised to find no bra, and she suddenly knew that *she obviously wasn't planning to stay dressed for very long tonight. The thought made her even more hungry.*

Remy felt Sarah's hand cup her breast and run over her nipple, the pressure making her hard. She deepened the kiss and cupped Sarah's bottom, pulling Sarah's hips against her aching clit. She eased her leg between Sarah's legs and ground into her clit, eliciting a deep moan. If Sarah was anywhere near as turned on as she was, her first orgasm was close. She ran her hand over Sarah's hips and eased her fingers under her waistband.

The aching need in Sarah's aroused core made her want to come out of her skin. She rode Remy's thigh, the seam of her jeans rubbing against her hardened clit and making it vibrate with pleasure. She needed to assuage the ache deep within. She pulled her hands from Remy's perfect body and opened her jeans, shoving Remy's hand into her panties. "I need you to touch me now." She didn't recognize her own voice. It came from somewhere outside her body. But it didn't matter, the voice gave life to her needs.

"Oh fuck, you're so wet." Remy ran her tongue over Sarah's neck and dipped inside her ear, sending shivers up and down Sarah's body.

Sarah was close, she could feel her muscles contracting around Remy's fingers and she closed her eyes, waiting for sweet release to overtake her.

Sarah jumped, a loud knocking waking her up. She looked past Parker, who was still sleeping and saw a state trooper peering in the window, motioning for them to roll down the window. She punched Parker in the leg and ducked when a hand came flying towards her face. "Wake up!"

Parker groaned loudly and eased the seat back up slowly. It wasn't till she saw Sarah's shocked expression that she looked to her left and saw a face looking back at her. "Oh shit!" She turned the key and fumbled with the buttons on the door till she found the window down button and pushed it, its decent painfully slow as though it were mocking her and trying to cause more trouble. "Officer?"

"Ladies." His tone was slightly amused. "Mind telling me what you're doing."

"Honestly, Officer, it's not what it looks like." Parker said quickly.

"Oh, so you're not sleeping together." He stated with a chuckle.

Sarah breathed a sigh of relief. They had actually gotten a trooper with a sense of humor. She leaned over Parker, grinding her elbow into her leg. She was rewarded with a loud groan. "This is my cousin and my driver. We're storm chasers. We are just waiting for the storms to hit."

"Reckon that's all right." The trooper took his hat off and scratched his head. "Might have made my day a bit more exciting if you had been sleeping together. But, since this is Oklahoma and not Kentucky, I'm sure glad you're not."

Sarah laughed. "Besides, her feet stink."

"Got one of them cousins myself. Not with stinky feet, he's an amateur chaser. Caught a funnel up to Medford 'bout a year ago."

"Oh yeah." Sarah replied excitedly. "We missed that one. We were stuck in Iowa. Good storm."

"Listen, I'm gonna let you girls go." The trooper offered. "Next time, try to find a safer spot to take a nap."

Parker finally got her wits about her and smiled. "Sure appreciate that Officer…Officer Cock." She managed to say it without a snicker.

He didn't respond for several seconds, and Parker was sure she had just gotten them back on trouble. Finally, he smiled and let her off the hook. "It's Koch, pronounced like cook. Fought that my whole life." He tapped the top of the car and walked away, his laughter echoing all the way back to his car.

"Holy hell!" Parker blew out a breath. "That was a close one."

"Tell me about it. And then you almost blow it by calling him a cock."

Parker shrugged. "Stop worrying. He wasn't going to do anything to this hotness."

Sarah snorted loudly. "Oh lord, I can't wait till someone tames you."

"Not gonna happen, Cuz." Parker said smugly. "I just finally found someone that could handle my gorgeous self."

"I think I just threw up in my mouth."

A gust of wind shook the car, and Sarah finally looked to her right. "Oh shit. It's here."

A massive mesocyclone had descended upon them and was turning rapidly. "Looks like you picked the right spot today." Parker offered. She pulled a small Nikon out of the back seat, leaned over Sarah and started snapping shots. "Oh man, it's really going. Look! Small rope funnel starting to form."

Sarah had the camera rolling. Her gut had been right again. "We've got another one. It's dropping another. See the tail."

Parker followed her finger and snapped pics as a larger rotation dropped out of the wall cloud. "The smaller one is dead. It's roping out, but that one looks like it will be massive. I see debris. It's on the ground."

The tornado looked to be several miles away, and at least a mile north of them, but Sarah kept her guard up. Tornadoes were known to turn on a dime. She had already been pulled into one, and she wasn't too keen on it happening again.

She pulled the map up and guessed where the tornado would track. Norman was directly in its path, and Oklahoma City wasn't far behind. She feared the worst, and knew that even the smallest window of warning could save lives. She pulled her phone out of her pocket and dialed 911. Moments later, she hung up, having warned the operator that at least one tornado was on the ground and heading for Norman.

By the time it hit, it was a full half—mile wide wedge tornado and the devastation was massive. By the time the intense trough was done, it dropped over sixty tornados through Oklahoma, Kansas and Missouri. It had leveled a trailer park and killed three in its merciless trek across the states.

Parker had faired a little better this time as they drove through parts of the damage. Like most people in high stress, high fatality jobs she was becoming desensitized. Sarah still felt immense grief and she could understand the passion that drove Remy. She would chase until she found a way to prevent any fatalities or the sweet kiss of death lighted upon her. Either way, Sarah knew that whatever else happened in her life, it would come second to her quest.

It was late when they finally pulled away from the city, having helped where they could and mourned with those that needed it. She could see the weight of it all in Parker's face and felt it in her own heart. She needed some respite to preoccupy her mind and block the images that haunted her, at least for a while.

"Call Carmen. Find out where they are and tell them we'll meet halfway."

Parker merely nodded, the smallest of smiles teasing the corner of her mouth as she dialed the number and waited for the voice she knew would calm her down.

Chapter 9

"...and then Parker calls him Officer Cock."

"Hey, it was an honest mistake. It was spelled K—O—C—H. How was I supposed to say it?"

Remy and Carmen couldn't contain their laughter. "Way to go, Parker." Remy teased. "My favorite is still you guys sleeping together. Kissing cousins, eh?"

"No." Sarah punched Remy in the arm. "I'd rather kiss you." She wished the words back the second she said them.

Remy caught her hand and her green eyes held Sarah's gaze, not allowing her to look away. "I'd much rather you kiss me too. Lucky you, we can arrange that."

Sarah could feel her cheeks getting hot, and she jerked her hand away. She looked down at her lap, but not before she caught the knowing wink that Parker shot her. She was the last person she wanted to know about her and Remy.

The waitress chose that moment to come to their table, saving her from further scrutiny. They had chosen a pizza joint just outside Wichita, Il Vicino. A small chain of wood oven pizzerias that Remy suggested they try. They each ordered a different pie and refills on their beers.

When the waitress left the table, Remy turned to Parker. "So, other than the run in with Smoky, how was your day? Ours was a complete bust. The storm dropped a small tornado about twenty miles north of us and we missed it."

Parker shrugged. "If you call three fatalities good, then we did alright."

"I know it is hard now." The concern was evident in her voice. "After a while, you sort of get numb to seeing it. You still feel awful, but it doesn't make you want to puke your guts out anymore."

"Well, that's comforting." Parker said sarcastically. "I don't know that I'm cut out for this."

Carmen squeezed her arm. "You'd be surprised what the human mind can tolerate when you have a goal in mind. Take Rem, for example. She's seen it all, but in the forefront is the desire to save as many people as possible, and that's what keeps her going."

"Oh, so a few lives lost for the greater good kind of thing."

"Not necessarily, but you don't lose sight of why you're out here when you focus on the real reason we do it." Carmen rubbed Parker's arm softly, trying to comfort her. "It's about remembering the people, but not necessarily picturing their deaths."

"It's not easy, Parker." Sarah smiled sadly. "I didn't mean to drag you into this."

"It's fine, Sarah. I just wasn't prepared for the pain that came with it. I always heard about the deaths on TV, but never witnessed them first hand. It's an adjustment."

"I'm sorry too, Parker." Remy said quickly. "I guess we have just been around longer so we forget what a newbie experiences their first few times. Let me tell you a story that might help you think about the positives. It was my first year out. Mind you, I had already witnessed tragedy most people don't see."

"Yeah, the EMT thing." Parker had overheard Remy telling Sarah why she got started chasing in the first place. It had seemed kind of crazy to her that she would want to trade in a job like that to do something as dangerous as chase tornadoes.

Remy nodded. "As rough as that was, nothing prepared me for the first year. There were so many times I almost gave up. I was young and brash, and I expected to come out and solve all the problems with forecasting tornadoes. I was going to save lives. But, the reality of it hit me pretty hard."

"Are you talking about Stockton?" Carmen asked in a serious tone. "That was bad."

Remy nodded at Carmen. "Stockton, Missouri, spring of 2003. It was a bad, bad season for tornadoes. We were following a trough that was working its way across the Midwest. By the time the system moved through, it had produced over 400 tornadoes all the way into Canada. For chasers, it was paradise. For everyone else, it was devastating. There were more than ninety people that lost their lives in less than a week."

Carmen nodded. "It was bad, Chica. But I promise there's a good part to this story."

"Two months into my first season, and we got hit with some of the worst weather I'd seen. Anyway, I told you this would help, so let me stop talking about how bad it was and get to the good part. We were driving west of Stockton when the storms got close. We had called 911, but it was dropping tornadoes faster than we had ever seen. There really wasn't a chance to get the warning out. We were driving through the main strip, and there was a school in session. We just knew the warning sirens would never go off in time. I was young and stupid and didn't realize there was a certain protocol for issuing the warnings. But, I would be damned if I was going to sit around and let a bunch of kids get hurt when there was a chance we could help. We stopped, ran to the office and told the principal that a line of strong storms was getting ready to hit Stockton and he needed to get everyone to safety."

"It ripped the roof off the school." Carmen said excitedly. "But, not one person was hurt."

"That does help some." Parker agreed. "Thank God you were there."

"Wait, it gets better." Remy smiled. "We stuck around after the tornado went through and helped anyway we could. The mom of one of the students ran up to me and threw her arms around me. She had two kids there and she had flipped out when the storm hit. When she found out her kids were okay, she started talking to the principal about how grateful she was that he was aware enough to get everyone into the bathrooms. He pointed her in my direction."

"Wow." Parker's voice was almost a whisper. "That had to feel good."

Remy brushed away tears. "I still can't talk about it without getting all choked up. I was ready to walk away. I couldn't take seeing town after town devastated. People left with nothing. But, when she hugged me and thanked me for saving her babies, I knew this was what I was meant to do. I couldn't turn my back on all those people. I had to accept that I may not save everyone, but even if I saved one life, it made my existence there worth it."

Sarah put her hand over Remy's arm. "You never told me that."

Remy shrugged. "You never asked. There's a lot I would tell you, if you were interested in hearing it."

Sarah pulled her hand away. It had merely been an observation, a comment made without censure, but it stung anyway. Had she really shut Remy so far out that she had never given her the opportunity to share her life? Parker saved her from responding, but her thoughts still bothered her.

"So, how did you deal with seeing your first…first dead body?" Parker swallowed a lump in her throat. She was trying to get past it, for Sarah anyway.

"The first couple of years, I got really good at forgetting, or at least filling my brain with something else." Remy was quiet a moment. "Carmen helped a lot."

"She did?"

"Uh-huh." Remy nodded and winked at Carmen. "She…umm…helped to get my mind off the harder parts of the job."

"Whoa! You two didn't sleep together, did you?" Parker's eyes narrowed.

Sarah leaned forward, suddenly very curious as to the answer. The answer shouldn't matter to her like it did to Parker, who was obviously now emotionally invested in Carmen, but she couldn't pass the sick feeling off as curiosity. Remy had mentioned that she wasn't attracted to Carmen and they hadn't slept together, but what if it hadn't been the truth.

Remy snorted loudly. "Me? Carmen?" She shook her head, her eyes dancing amusedly. "No way. We've always been more like sisters than anything else. Let's just say she came up with some activities that helped take the edge off."

Sarah let out the breath she had been holding. She knew it was foolish to let something like that bother her. She knew Remy had shared a bed with multiple partners over the years, and she was just another notch on her belt, or she thought she was. Her conversation with Remy a few days earlier was still running through her mind, opening doors that she had thought closed. "So, what did you two get into?"

Their waitress, as if sensing the need to intervene and save Remy from answering, picked that moment to bring their food out. The smell coming from the food was so enticing that the earlier conversation was momentarily forgotten. They were four friends united by a cause, thankful for the chance to be part of something greater than each one of them alone.

Chapter 10

Sarah opened the door without even looking and sat back on the bed.

Remy quirked an eyebrow and came inside chuckling. "Expecting me, huh?"

"Given the fact that they couldn't keep their hands off each other, I'm surprised they made it past the car."

"True." Remy held out a bottle of wine. "Wine?"

Sarah leaned forward and checked the label. "Cab? Nothing like your wine bighting you back."

Remy took the teasing in stride, a small smirk on her face. She pulled her arm from behind her back and handed Sarah another bottle. "Better?"

"Mmm, pinot. Now, you are talking." Sarah grabbed a couple of plastic cups off the bathroom sink. "These okay?"

Remy shrugged. "Either that or just chug."

"I think I'll suffer with the cup." Sarah looked around confusion on her face. Her eyebrows furrowed, and Remy was forced to admit that she was quite cute when she was presented with a conundrum.

Remy pulled a small wine opener from her back pocket and waggled it in front of Sarah's face. "You didn't think I was going to offer wine and not come prepared, did you?"

"Maybe." Sarah admitted with a blush. "I should have known better."

Remy opened both bottles and poured them a glass. She took hers and sat on the opposite bed. They sat for several moments without talking. The day had finally caught up with them. Decompressing often consisted of long moments of silence, rather than rehashing the details, allowing them to unwind and finally relax.

"This is good, thank you." Sarah smiled sweetly.

A loud bang on the wall made them both jump. Remy smirked. "I might have to rethink this whole rooms being together thing. I don't know about Parker, but Carmen can go for hours. I may be here awhile."

Sarah shrugged her shoulders. "It's okay. I figure I need to let Parker blow off steam. I didn't realize this would be so hard on her."

"It's harder on some people." Remy leaned her head against the wall and sighed. "What about you? How did you take your first time?"

"It was bad, but not like it was for Parker." Sarah replied. She stopped to pour herself another glass and sank back down. "I watched my brother die in front of me."

"What?" Remy's brow furrowed. "I didn't know that."

"Not many people outside of my family do."

"What happened…if you don't mind me asking."

"Hunting accident." Sarah swiped her eyes.

"It's okay, we don't have to talk about it." Remy offered.

"No, no, I'm fine. Some days are just harder than others. It's that time of the month, and I'm always more emotional then."

Remy nodded knowingly. "I know exactly what you mean." She sat quietly waiting for Sarah to start talking again.

"Deer." Sarah offered after a while. "The town I grew up in was about an hour from Nashville. My family hunted for as long as I can remember. It was never a question that once we hit the age we could fire a rifle that we would join everyone else. My brother was a couple of years older than me, so he had been hunting for at least six years when it happened. There was a small reserve north of us that my dad suggested we try." The more she talked the more her voice trembled.

Remy joined her on the bed and grabbed her hand to comfort her. "You don't have to tell me."

"No, I think I need too. I never talked about it after that day. My family was what you call emotionally closed off. We didn't talk about it. We didn't really grieve in front of anyone. My dad had always been the guy that taught us it was only sissies that cried. We didn't show emotion."

"That had to have been hard." Remy squeezed her hand.

"God, it was. I was thirteen and I couldn't even mourn my brother's passing. We just went about our lives. The only thing my dad did to acknowledge that it happened was hanging my brother's rifle in his room. No one was allowed to use it after that day."

"I don't know how you did it. My family, we are criers. Even my dad."

Sarah chuckled softly, thankful for something to lighten the mood. "I find that hard to believe. Somehow, I don't see you tearing up at the latest Hallmark commercial."

"Well, it's actually the On Star commercials, but you get the idea."

"Thank you." Sarah smiled, laughter in her voice. "I needed that." She took a sip of her wine. "Anyway, it was the last day of the hunt and we had only gotten one small buck, a four point that my uncle shot. My brother didn't want to leave without getting something. He went off without us, which wasn't out of the norm for him. He was kind of a loner even then. There was another group in the valley he chose, a bunch of guys that had come in from the city to *experience* the whole wildlife thing." Sarah said acerbically. "My brother had taken off his vest, for whatever reason we won't ever know. One of the guys saw movement and assumed it was a deer. He shot my brother and pierced a lung."

"Holy shit."

"By the time that they tracked us down, it was too late. There was no way we could get him out in time. I just remember his head resting in my lap, watching the life drain from him. It was the hardest thing I've ever had to do. The thing that got to me the most was with his last breath, he said 'I love you, Sis'. We never said we loved each other, we didn't talk about feelings. I will remember those words as long as I live."

Remy got off the bed, got a Kleenex and handed it to Sarah without a word. She was humbled. Sarah had opened up and let her in, sharing a part of herself. The tragedy that had helped shape who she was. She waited, allowing her to cry, merely offering her shoulder as comfort.

Several moments passed before Sarah sniffed and smiled weakly at Remy. "Thank you."

"For making you relive something that horrific." Remy said with self—recrimination.

"No. For letting me talk about it. Every day of my life, I miss my brother more than I can imagine. But, I kept it all locked inside, never having anyone to talk to about it." Sarah felt relief and her shoulders felt lighter than they had in years, the weight of her brother's death not as heavy a burden as it had been. It hadn't just been opening up that helped, it seemed to her that she had actually taken a piece of her grief and handed it to Remy, who silently accepted every bit of it. "It means more to me than you will ever know."

Remy pulled Sarah tighter against her body. The warmth between them was something foreign to her. She had become emotionally invested in the woman beside her. It was no longer physical hunger that made her long for Sarah, her heart had started to yearn for her. She had never wanted more than sex with anyone, and these new feelings of longing scared her. She wasn't sure how to deal with the quickening of her pulse, the thoughts of a future shared with only one person. This was new, uncharted territory, and Remy sensed that in order to deal with whatever evolution she was undergoing, she was going to have to stop thinking with her libido and start thinking with her heart.

Sarah sensed the change in Remy immediately. She felt her body tighten against hers and she knew she should put distance between them, but she couldn't. She needed the comfort she was offering. She set her cup on the nightstand and met Remy's questioning gaze. "Can I ask you something and you not take it the wrong way?"

Remy's brow furrowed. "Sure?" She asked, her reservations quickly surfacing. There was no way that the question would be harmless, and given her current state, whatever Sarah was asking was probably outside what she would normally be comfortable with.

"Will you stay with me…at least till I fall asleep?" Sarah yawned behind her hand.

Remy could only nod. Something in her request was more intimate than actually making love would have been. She reached over Sarah, put her cup on the table and flipped the light off.

Sarah lay down on the bed and snuggled against Remy, pulling her arm around her stomach. Their breathing slowed till the only sound in the room was the ticking of the clock on the wall. She needed to sleep, but the feeling of being in Remy's arms was like a drug and she wanted to bask in it a while longer. "Thank you."

Remy barely heard the whisper above her heartbeat, and had she not been pressed against Sarah, she may have missed it. She didn't feel the need to respond other than to pull Sarah tightly against her.

Hours later, Remy was still awake, listening to Sarah's even breathing. Somewhere in the span of the night, her heart had opened up and let Sarah in. Her chest tightened when she thought of them together, knowing that Sarah did not return her feelings. With a sigh, she slid off the bed, careful not to wake Sarah. She paused at the door, her eyes finding Sarah's face in a thin sliver of light. Suddenly, she was no longer merely chasing storms, she was chasing love.

Chapter 11

Remy watched a hail—battered Chevy pull up to the pump next to hers, and a smile broke out on her face. She had left Sarah hours before, but she could feel warmth where Sarah had been tucked against her like it was only minutes before. She waited until Sarah noticed her and a knowing look passed between them.

Sarah couldn't help but smile. She felt a hundred times lighter today than she had yesterday, and the beautiful woman standing across the pump from her was mostly responsible for the change. "You've really got to stop stalking me like this. People are going to think you like me or something."

Remy quirked an eyebrow. "Or, something." She stepped closer and held Sarah's gaze. "You okay this morning?"

Sarah nodded. "I'm better…thanks to you." She admitted begrudgingly.

Remy could tell the admission cost Sarah some of her pride. "It was nothing really. Just helping a friend out."

"Is that what we are?" Sarah's forehead wrinkled in thought.

"I'd like to think so." Remy looked hopeful. "I know we have a history, and you made it perfectly clear you would rather not have it, and hope to never repeat it, but I hope you can put that aside and at least pretend to like me."

Sarah couldn't ignore her crooked smile. She reminded her of a little kid looking for acceptance. She also couldn't ignore her heart skipping a beat when Remy smiled at her. She liked her alright, probably too much for her own comfort. In truth, she had taken advantage of Remy last night. She knew if she asked Remy to stay, there would be no way she could say no. It wasn't fair, she shouldn't have used her that way, but Sarah had needed her strength and her serenity. It calmed her somewhere deep inside, a place that had been unsettled for as long as she could remember. It scared her. Remy had managed to get inside her like no one else had, and she wasn't sure she would be able to keep her emotional distance.

"So, I'm going to take the silence as a yes?" Remy teased.

"Oh yeah." Sarah shook her head. "Sorry. Yes, I can't say I don't like you."

A smile broke out on Remy's face that spread from ear to ear. "Okay, good. I was about to run crying to Carmen and she's a little preoccupied at the moment."

Sarah followed Remy's gaze and laughed. Sure enough, while their attention was focused on each other, Carmen had grabbed Parker, and they were huddled on the side of the gas station in the middle of a very passionate kiss. "Jeez, would they get a room?"

"Preferably together." Remy shook her head from side to side. "That way maybe I won't get kicked out of my room every night."

Sarah's gaze fixed on Remy. "I thought you liked getting kicked out."

"Umm, I would prefer it if…" Remy paused, her face suddenly warm. "…I'd actually like it if someone wanted to share a room with me, and I'm not talking about C."

"Oh." Sarah replied, realization dawning in her features. "You mean…"

Remy smiled, her eyes locked on Sarah's. "Yes." She didn't need to give voice to her thoughts. They both knew what she meant. She had made it perfectly clear that she was still interested in Sarah and thought they might have a future together if Sarah got out of her own way and gave them a chance. For now, she would settle for friendship with the secret hope of more. Somehow, in the grand scheme of things, someone had worked it out that Sarah and Remy were never far apart. And, in an even bigger twist of fate, Carmen and Parker were practically throwing them together.

"Remy, I..." Sarah spoke feebly. "I..."

Remy put her hand on her arm to stop her. "I know, Sarah. You're only interested in friendship. I have never been sorry for that night until now. Had I known that was my one chance with you, I would have run the other way. It's only now that I can finally appreciate that no matter how amazing that night was, it wasn't worth losing the chance of a future with you."

Sarah felt a pain in her chest. She was trying hard to remain aloof, but Remy said things that made her feel again. She was treading dangerous waters with Remy. She knew if she let go, she would fall for her, and fall hard, and that was not a risk she was willing to take. "I'm sorry, Remy. I can't be more than your friend. Please let that be enough."

"It is." *For now.* Remy thought. She took a step back, putting necessary space between them. She broke the connection between them, her eyes finding Carmen again. "I think we better get those two under control before they are arrested for public indecency."

Sarah laughed, thankful that Remy had let her off the hook. "I'll get mine and kick yours over here at the same time." She jogged over to the couple lost in their embrace and punched Parker playfully.

Remy watched Sarah across the parking lot and her heart skipped a beat. Her words were very different from what her eyes were saying. Remy had gotten very good at reading people and what she saw in Sarah was fear. Not of Remy, but of herself. Sarah was afraid of her feelings for Remy and denial was her protection. Remy smiled. *Deny all you want, darling. I'm not going anywhere, and sooner or later, you will realize that you love me too.*

Carmen walked back to the truck with a sheepish grin on her face that turned into a full blown blush when she saw the look Remy was giving her. "What?"

"Don't what me, you know."

"Oh, that? That was nothing." Carmen grabbed the hose off the pump and shoved it into Thor's large tank.

"Really? 'Cause what it looked like was you trying to give Parker a tonsillectomy in the middle of a parking lot."

Carmen snorted. "Funny, Chica."

Remy rolled her eyes and got back into the truck. She tried stealing glances of Sarah, but the large metal plates around the truck impeded her view. She didn't need to see her face though. Sarah's image was etched in her mind, and no amount of time had been able to erase it from her memory. Last night still played in her mind. Sarah's body had fit perfectly against hers, and in her sleep, she had lost her inhibitions. Her soft bottom pressed into Remy's core and ignited sparks that lit through her body.

Lying with Sarah had felt right, more right than any feeling she'd ever had before. There was a perfectness to their closeness, uniting them even more than the hurried sex they had so many years before. Remy had always been attracted to Sarah. She was gorgeous. But, now she was getting to know her and her heart was involved. This was more than she had ever given to anyone, and now when she wanted to share it, it had been rejected. That was the hardest part of her infatuation with Sarah—that it wasn't returned.

Carmen hopped in the truck and slammed the door. "Where to, Chica?"

"Gosh, I don't know." Remy said sarcastically. "Where's your girlfriend headed?"

Carmen shrugged. "Not sure. Parker said whatever direction you headed, Sarah was driving the opposite way."

So, that was how this was going to be. I get too close, and she bolts the other way. "She's funny."

"Yeah, she is." Carmen looked out the window and watched the Chevy drive away. "Guess that means we oughta head the other way."

Remy shook her head and peeled out as fast as a five—ton truck would allow her to. "Nope. Two can play this game."

She turned the truck onto the highway in the same direction Sarah had taken only minutes before. She would just keep the speed a little slower, which wasn't hard given Sarah's proclivity for speed. Normally, she would run the other way, not caring to make a point, but today was different. She could feel Sarah trying to close the door she had just opened.

Carmen watched Remy, an amused smile on her face. If she didn't know better, she would swear that she had a thing for Sarah, even though she would never admit it. Carmen was no fool. She had seen the looks that passed between them, the connection that joined them even when they thought no one else was watching. Remy wouldn't admit to it, but Carmen had a sneaking suspicion when she and Parker wanted some privacy, Remy found her way to Sarah's hotel room. What they did, she wasn't sure, but she could almost bet it didn't include the same activities that she and Parker participated in. That thought brought a small smirk to her lips.

Remy fought the urge to break the law in order to close the gap between the two vehicles. She was certain Sarah hadn't figured out yet that they were heading in the same direction. If she had, she probably would have forced Remy to pull over and given her what for. Remy managed to ease off the gas pedal, knowing out here there weren't many roads Sarah could turn on that she wouldn't be able to follow.

"Chica?" Carmen asked, amusement in her tone. "Whatcha up to?"

Remy smiled sheepishly. "Nada. Just driving."

"I can see that. What I mean is what is going on? With you and Sarah? I've never seen a woman get under your skin like she does."

"She's not." Remy said defensively. "I just figured that since we struck out yesterday, maybe we ought to give her tracking skills a chance."

"Mmm—hmmm, and all of a sudden mine aren't good enough?"

"That's not what I meant and you know it." Remy fidgeted in her seat, uncomfortable at being caught red—handed. "Oh fine, whatever." She caught the questioning look in Carmen's eyes and knew she was done. "Tell me where to go."

Carmen chuckled softly. "Might as well keep heading this direction. For right now, I'm thinking the same thing she is. There's a line of storms moving over the Rockies. It should hit Iowa sometime late this afternoon. That's about the only thing going on in the next couple of days."

"Then Iowa here we come. Guess Sarah will just have to deal with it." And it seemed that was just what she was intending to do. She had pulled Chevy Chase off the road and was standing against the back of the car with her arms crossed over her chest. Fortunately, Remy was coming up over a slight hill and her speed had slowed considerably. "Looks like I'm about to get it."

When Remy braked behind Sarah's car, she turned the engine off and shrugged her shoulders at Carmen. She could see Sarah striding towards the car and the glare on her face let Remy know very quickly she was not excited to see her. She stepped out timidly and met her on the shoulder of the road.

"What the hell are you doing?" Sarah asked loudly.

Remy smiled ruefully and wished she could slink back to the truck and run in the opposite direction. She thought Sarah's head might actually start to spin. "Just following a lead."

"Really? And it just happens to be the same direction I'm headed?"

"You've seen the map, Bonneville. You know there's nothing out there except for the storm you're going to."

Calling her Bonneville at that particular moment was probably not the safest thing to do. Sarah could feel the heat rise in her neck. She shouldn't be so upset with the nickname, or the fact that Remy had chosen the same storm. She was more frustrated with herself. She could put physical distance between them, but it was the emotional distance she wanted and couldn't achieve. No, she had finally accepted that no matter how far away she ran, Remy would always be there, buried in the dark recesses of her mind and slowly working her way into her heart. "It's mine, Remy."

"Oh, we are calling dibs on the storms now?" Remy's eyes danced with laughter.

"Ooh!" Sarah's body shook with barely concealed irritation. "Why do you have to get under my skin?"

"Funny, I was thinking the same about you." Remy confessed.

"What do you mean? I don't do anything to irritate you."

"No, no, you don't." Remy moved closer to Sarah and licked her lips. "You get under my skin in an entirely different way."

Sarah's mouth dropped in shock. She opened and closed it several times and still couldn't manage to utter a word. Truth be told, Remy had gotten to her a long time ago, she just didn't have the nerve to admit it. Especially not to Remy. "Fine. Do whatever you want. Just don't get in my way."

Remy shrugged. "No problem. Iowa's a big state." She turned on her heal and strode back to the truck, leaving Sarah standing there mouth agape. She pulled the door open and stopped with her foot on the door ledge. "Good luck, Bonneville."

She broke into laughter when Sarah's only reaction was to flip her the bird over her right shoulder. When she got in, she met Carmen's amused stare. "Well, that went better than I thought."

"How's that? You look like you barely escaped with your head."

"She didn't slap me, and that's more than I can say for some women I've met."

"Met or slept with?"

Remy felt the heat rise in her face. She knew Carmen could read the telltale signs of her guilt. She couldn't respond and not give the truth away. Rather than acknowledge the question, Remy started the truck and eased back into traffic and shook her head. Today was going to be a long damn day.

Chapter 12

Seven hours later they crossed the Nebraska—Iowa border and Remy yawned loudly. "I don't know about you, but I got to hit the can."

Carmen checked the radar. "Make it fast. There's a supercell about fifty miles west of here and it's going to hit south of Sioux City. We've got a ways to go."

Remy followed the sign to a rest area and pulled Thor into one of the semi parking spots. She got out and stretched her arms over her head. Normally, it didn't bother her to be in the car for hours on end, but today her emotions were frayed, and she was having a hard time relaxing. She was stiff and sore and slightly irritated. Carmen had picked up on it and wisely chosen to take a nap, or at least pretend to. "You going?"

Carmen shook her head and followed her across the parking lot. She sniffed the air around her. It smelled like miles and miles of farmland tinted with fresh air and a hint of rain blown in by the sweet Great Plains wind. She inhaled deeply, appreciating the world around her. It was at times like this, she felt as though she was one with nature, her connection to Mother Nature honing her skill at chasing storms. She followed Remy into the restroom and immediately wished she was back outside.

Besides a couple of words, they hadn't spoken most of the long ride from Oklahoma to Iowa, which didn't particularly suit Carmen. She liked conversation. Coming from a big family who wasn't quiet in the least, she sometimes missed the noisy camaraderie she shared with her Latin family. For the most part, Remy was good at filling the quiet in between, but days like today, when she was introspective were tough and made Carmen miss her family. "So, Chica, can we talk now?"

Remy shook her head ruefully. "I'm sorry, C. Bad day, and I shouldn't have taken it out on you."

"Si, you shouldn't have." Carmen punched her arm playfully. "I know what your problem is."

"Oh yeah?" Remy quirked an eyebrow. "Do tell, oh wise one."

"You need to get laid." Carmen stated matter—of—fact. "You're wound tighter than a nun in a nudist colony."

Remy snorted. Carmen had a way of making up things that were just different enough from the actual phrase that they often left Remy in stitches. "You just make that up?"

"No, no, of course not." Carmen waived her hand dismissively. "I hear that all the time."

"You know it doesn't count if you hear it in Spanglish."

"Lo que sea!" Carmen put her palm up in the air and rolled her eyes.

"Don't whatever me." Remy teased. "I might lock you in the hotel room tonight."

Carmen smirked. "No, you won't."

"You don't think so?" Remy narrowed her eyes.

"No, Chica, I don't. If I stay in the room, then you don't get to spend the evening with Sarah."

Remy frowned. Carmen did have a point. As much as she didn't want to admit it, Remy had to accept that it was true. If Carmen didn't kick her out of the room every night, she would probably have sat in the room or found a bar somewhere and drank. Honestly, she preferred Sarah's company and liked the excuse to spend her nights there. "Just tell me if the storm is heading this way."

Carmen snorted. "I think you've already run into the storm, Chica." She pulled her phone out and pulled the radar up, her laughter filling the truck. She knew that whatever was happening between Remy and Sarah was bringing out the tempest in Sarah, and she was secretly glad that was a storm she wasn't dealing with. "'Kay, it's making its way through Nebraska. I figure it will hit here in another hour or so. Could be a good one. There's already some small supercells developing and there's definitely a hook echo at the southern tip."

"Guess we better get moving." Remy headed back out to I—29 and followed it a short time before turning onto Highway 37 near Onawa. She flicked her eyes towards Carmen's phone trying to see the storm. It was small, but she could make out the hook pattern near the tip and knew if there was going to be a tornado, it would spawn near that point. "So, what's the deal with you and Parker? Moving kind of fast, eh?"

Carmen smirked. "Not so fast for you, though."

"Forget fast lately, I haven't gotten any action at all." Remy shook her head. "You still *walking down the aisle, three kids, living in the suburbs* serious?"

"Pretty much." Carmen blushed. "I know it is fast, and normally, I would worry, but not with Parker. I feel like I know the real her, and I know my heart."

"Your heart or your libido?" Remy teased. "Sure you aren't letting other parts of your body do the talking?"

"Funny. At least I'm letting my body talk."

"Oh good, now we're quoting Olivia Newton John." Remy broke out into the chorus of *Let's Get Physical*, teasing Carmen mercilessly. She felt the tension slowly start to ebb away. Carmen was right though, she needed to get some action. She was wound tighter than a two—dollar watch. *And that's how you use a cliché.*

At least the last hour was passing more quickly than the rest of the drive had. They hit 175 before she knew it, and the outskirts of Mapleton weren't far away. Remy smiled when she saw a navy Chevy in the distance, an attractive blonde perched on the hood.

"I don't think she's happy to see you, Chica." Carmen said with a chuckle.

Remy had gathered as much from the glare she got when they drove by. She picked a spot about a quarter mile up the road and pulled the truck over. She pulled her gear out of the truck and rested against the door. "Think it's going to drop?"

Carmen eyed the massive shelf cloud that was moving over the plain. "God, if it doesn't, I'd be shocked." She flicked her head towards the direction they had just come. "Figure if it does, I hope we get better footage than the competition."

Remy eyed Sarah's car in the rear view mirror. "Still gets me that she got the footage from inside the twister. The best we got is still outrunning one."

"Guess we could get a little crazy today." Carmen winked. "Feel like going for a ride?"

Remy could see from Carmen's smile she was only half—joking. "You're serious? After you reamed me out the last time? If I do, I'm leaving your ass standing on the side of the road at least a mile away."

"Yeah, but last time I didn't have an audience."

"You've got to be kidding me." Remy said sarcastically. "Because your woman is watching, you're willing to throw yourself into the path of danger."

Carmen stood up proudly and her next words were heavily—accented. "For de woman, I will take a bullet."

Remy busted out laughing. "You, my dear, are so pussy—whipped, it is not even funny."

"At least I'm getting some." Carmen answered wickedly. "So, are we doing this or not? I need to mentally prepare."

Remy eyed the darkening sky overhead. "Start taking some deep breaths, we are about to dance with the devil."

Carmen felt the wind pick up and the telltale chill roll across her body, and she knew something was about to happen. She started clicking pictures of the large shelf cloud, looking for signs of rotation. "There, there! Look at the rotation in that mesocyclone."

Remy watched the rapid movement of the clouds through her video camera. The first drops of rain pelted against the truck, smattering against her body and making her shiver. "It's dropping. We've got a small funnel dropping out of the storm. We've got debris." She picked up her cell phone and dialed the emergency operator. She cupped her hand over the phone, trying to hear over the wind. "Shit! We've got another one. Hello? Yes, this is Remy Tate. I am on 175 just south of Mapleton. We have a multi—vortex tornado southwest of the city. It's tracking right for Mapleton." She hung up the phone and looked behind her, hoping this time Sarah played it safe.

"Come on, Rem. It's growing fast. We gotta get moving. We need to intercept it." Carmen jumped back in the truck and leaned over Remy, shooting pictures of the rapidly moving tornado.

Remy started the truck and shot back out on the highway. The tornado had wedged out and was pushing a half—mile wide. Soon they were running neck and neck with the massive funnel. "This is it. You ready?"

Carmen had put the camera down and strapped herself in, her hands gripped the seat beneath her. She gave Remy a shaky grin. "Let's do this, Chica."

Sarah's mouth dropped in shock. "What the fuck is she doing?"

Parker's eyes narrowed in on Thor and she felt a chill roll over her body. "She wouldn't?"

"Is she crazy?" Sarah couldn't believe what she was seeing. Remy was actually driving towards the tornado, with every intention of intercepting it. "God, Remy, please don't be stupid."

Remy slowed considerably. She'd been this close before, but it was always moving the opposite direction, running from the twister, not into it. She shook off second thoughts, knowing as risky as it was, they would gather much needed data deep within the storm. She knew it was better than dropping a probe or shooting small weather planes into the funnel.

Sarah squinted, trying to see the truck through the raindrops and the massive swirl of wind and debris. They were lost at least visually. Her heart dropped into her stomach. "I'm going to kill her if she makes it out alive."

Parker grabbed her hand. "They'll be alright. But, if they aren't and something happens to Carmen, I'll kill her too!"

Remy could feel the winds, from what she guessed was an EF3 tornado, start to batter them around, the outer bands threatening to rip Thor off the road. Her breath was coming in short, rapid spurts, and she could feel her heart hammering against her chest. "Shit, shit, shit!"

The funnel had grown to three-quarters of a mile wide and was barreling down on the small town of Mapleton, and in its path, was Thor and its rather unsettled occupants.

Remy had a death grip on the steering wheel with one hand, and her other hand shielded her face from the debris that was being kicked up and thrown at them at over one hundred miles an hour. The small bits of dirt and sand stung the hell out of her face and she was tempted to roll the window up, but didn't in case the hail started to fall.

She shoved the video camera at Carmen, forcing her to release her grip and take it. "Keep filming. This was your idea, remember."

"Remind me what a tanta I am for suggesting this." Carmen said over the din.

The truck rattled around them. The winds had almost doubled the closer they got to the tornado. Remy looked left and deciding they were close enough that the tornado would pass over them, pulled over and pushed a button to lower heavy steal pieces that would anchor the truck to the ground and hopefully keep them from getting ripped off their mooring.

The debris was too much and she was forced to roll up the window. Fortunately, the hail was only small, golf ball size pieces. Her fear now was getting hit by a large piece of debris or tree that the storm had ripped out of the ground.

"Oh fuck!" Carmen ducked instinctively. A large branch slammed against the truck and veered off just as quickly. "Que Dios, me ayude!"

"Hey, what about me?" Remy shouted.

Carmen crossed her chest and shrugged. "I'll try, Chica, but I don't think God likes me enough to save both of us."

Remy swatted Carmen's arm. Even in danger, they were at odds. They were like sisters. She felt the truck rattle dangerously, and she grabbed the doorframe. "God damn it!"

Carmen looked at her askance. "Kinda working against me here."

"Sorry." Remy threw a cross over her chest in an attempt to help. "Holy shit! I can't see a thing, but I think we are moving."

Carmen stilled and felt it too. Thor was inching sideways. "Oh shit, shit, we are moving! It's spinning us around."

They could feel the truck threatening to lift off the ground, the sheer energy of the wind around them almost too much for the anchors. Not able to make out anything in front of them, they could only tell they were moving from the queasiness in their stomachs.

Remy's face was gray, and she felt her stomach jump. "Are you getting this? Are you getting this?"

"I got it! I got it!" Carmen shouted. The camera was shaking in her hands, and she hoped the anti—shake feature actually worked or the footage would be worthless. It would just be a gray screen and the two of them shouting loudly.

Remy felt the truck come to a stop with a small shiver. "It's passing over. I think we made it."

Carmen kept the camera pointed out the window till the tornado was well over them. She could see it dissipating on what she knew to be the northeast side of Mapleton. She hoped her hands had stopped shaking enough to keep the playback steady. Up till moments ago, they hadn't been able to see anything past the first few feet out of the window, their view obscured by the tornado and the debris it tossed about without care.

Their first view of the town was utter devastation. Remy's jaw dropped in disbelief. Over half the small town was leveled. Remy tried to drive into the town, but she was flagged down by a sheriff.

"Chaser's, huh?" She asked as her eyes flicked over Thor's steal hull. "You the one that called the tornado in?"

Remy shook her head. A silent understanding had passed between them the second the sheriff walked up to the window, but this wasn't the time for either one to act on it. "Yeah, picked it up just southwest of the town."

"Sure do appreciate that. Best as I can tell, there are only injuries, no fatalities. Could have been a totally different story, though. Heard Pocahontas took an EF4. Didn't lose one person…luckily." She tipped her hat and started back towards her car. Turning around, she held Remy's gaze a moment before she spoke again. "You'll want to head back out the way you came. We're closing the city because of the damage."

Remy nodded, knowing it would be useless to try and get around. Besides, there wasn't much she and Carmen could have done anyway. "You're welcome."

Chapter 13

Parker ran towards Thor, anger flashing in her features. She flew at Remy and shouted a slew of cuss words in her face.

Remy backed up, confusion on her face. "What the hell?"

Parker pointed a finger in her face. "Are you nuts? You could have gotten her killed."

"Gotten who killed?" Remy stood her ground, her gaze leveled on Parker.

"Calm down, Parker." Carmen put her hand on Parker's arm. "We're okay."

"No thanks to her." She glared at Remy. "You could have gotten Carmen killed. You can't just go around doing whatever you want and putting people's lives in danger. What if something happened to the woman I love?"

Carmen stopped dead in her tracks. "You love me?"

Parker stilled and met Carmen's gaze. "I do. I'm sorry, that's a crappy way to tell you, but yes. I love you."

Carmen's lip quivered and she threw her arms around Parker. "I don't care how you tell me. I love you too. Te amo."

Remy shook her head, women she thought. Can't live with them, can't shoot 'em. "Wasn't even my idea."

Neither woman heard her muttered words or saw her backing away from them. Remy pulled the truck door open and was about to get back in when Sarah hit Remy in the arm.

"Are you fucking crazy? Why on earth would you drive straight into a tornado?" She was furious, but Remy picked up on the concern buried underneath.

"You did it." Remy said defensively.

"Not on purpose." Sarah's nostrils flared angrily. "I would never endanger myself or my team that way."

Remy smiled ruefully. "I'm sorry. Scared I wouldn't make it and you wouldn't get another night with me?"

Sarah eyes narrowed. "What I'm scared of is some rookie gets a hold of the footage and decides that's the cool thing to do. I'm scared that Parker finally finds someone she is willing to put her player card aside for and you risk her life."

Remy closed the space between them till she could feel the heat coming from Sarah's body. "But, you weren't worried about me at all?"

Sarah gulped, trying to swallow the lump in her throat. She wanted to believe that she didn't care, but the jump in her stomach told her otherwise. When she spoke, her voice shook nervously. "No."

Remy held her gaze. She had hoped for the same reaction that Carmen had received from Parker, but something told her that Sarah wasn't about to lock lips with her in the parking lot. That didn't keep her from letting Sarah know what she wanted. "I'm not going anywhere, Bonneville." She watched the color rise in Sarah's cheeks. She knew she shouldn't tease like she did, but it was so much fun getting under her skin. "You could keep me safe, you know."

Sarah shook her head, not understanding.

"Ask me not to do it again." Remy whispered softly. "You know I would do anything you ask me."

Sarah backed up, trying to break the connection, but she couldn't free herself of Remy's intense gaze. She suddenly wondered if there was a legitimate reason why she refused to sleep with her. She couldn't come up with one, other than her standby. She had made the mistake once and didn't want to repeat it for fear of getting hurt. "I can't."

Remy shrugged. "Then I guess we are at an impasse."

Sarah was saved from responding by Parker's shout. "Come on, I'm starving."

"Oh what, your make out session is done, so we all have to jump." Remy said wryly.

Parker laid her arm on Carmen's shoulder and grinned. "Yeah, today, it's all about me."

Remy followed them into the restaurant, her eyes glued to Sarah's shapely bottom. She found herself wishing she could cup it in her hands and bring Sarah's clit into her mouth.

When she walked through the door, Parker smirked at her.

"Nice view?"

"Uh, yeah." Remy managed to stutter.

Sarah looked at the menu and nudged Parker. "Coney Island Wiener House. Really?"

"Best weiner in town." Parker teased. "And, they say lesbians don't like wiener."

Remy groaned loudly and turned to Carmen. "Can you put a leash on your pet?"

Carmen laughed and threaded her arm through Parker's. "There's no taming her. And, she does have a point. I am particularly fond of her weiner."

"Is that so?" Remy smirked. "You packing, Parker?"

"Yeah, maybe."

Sarah watched them, a look of confusion on her face. "What are you guys talking about? Packing?"

Parker coughed nervously, her eyes pleading with Remy. "Can you help a brother out?"

"Hey, you strapped your problem on, now deal with it."

"Come on, Remy. Just tell me."

Remy found the lost look in her eyes very endearing, and she had to force herself to stop staring. She pulled Sarah towards her and leaned into her. Her hair brushed Remy's nose and she got lost in her scent. Sarah smelled like rain and summer, two of Remy's favorite smells. She inhaled deeply, getting momentarily lost. Finally, getting herself together, she whispered in Sarah's ear.

Sarah's eyes dropped to Parker's crotch and her mouth dropped in shock. She turned towards Remy. "You mean?"

Remy shook her head. "Yep."

"And, women like that?" Sarah couldn't quite wrap her head around the thought that a lesbian would like dick.

"Yeah, they do actually." Remy leaned in again and whispered. *"I could show you sometime."*

Sarah felt her body shutter. She wouldn't have thought her body would react this way, but she felt her loins tighten up and her heart start to pound.

"It's all about penetration. And, trust me, Bonneville, you would love it." Remy nuzzled Sarah's ear before she pulled away. She was pushing it, she knew, but Sarah had her so damn worked up that all the blood in her body seemed to be pooled between her legs. She could feel the seam of her jeans pressing against her clit and it twitched violently.

Sarah coughed nervously. "I...I...that's not necessary. I can assure you, that isn't something I'm into."

Carmen put her fingers on her arm and smiled. "I don't mean to push, but I can promise you, once you have it, it's something you will definitely be into." She squeezed Parker's arm and smiled lasciviously. "Especially when your girl works it the right way. And, apparently all that hot—dogging today, pardon the pun, has got her hard for me."

Sarah nearly choked. If she wasn't picturing Remy inside her before, she certainly was now. Desperate to clear the image from her mind, she stepped up to the counter, ending any further discussion about wieners and packing and whatever else they had called it.

Parker met Remy's eyes and shook her head. "My cousin, she's a little uptight."

"It's cool. I like tight." Remy replied with a smirk.

Once they were seated and halfway through chili dogs and Cokes, Remy chuckled softly at Sarah. "You should have seen your face."

"What?"

"When I told you about packing. You looked like you had just shown up naked at the senior prom."

"Not funny, Remy." Sarah said sarcastically, but there was a smile in her eyes.

"I didn't mean to embarrass you."

"You didn't, just threw me a little. Believe me, that was not embarrassed and I know embarrassment."

Carmen's ears perked up. "Ooh, someone has a story. Do tell."

"Nothing as bad as Parker." Sarah saw Parker go red, and she laughed out loud. "You know what I'm talking about."

Parker smiled wickedly. "Yeah, and what half our graduating class was talking about."

"Go Huskies!" They shouted in unison then dissolved into laughter.

"Okay, okay, okay." Parker waved her hand in the air. "Let me start out by saying this particular prom night had only a slight wardrobe malfunction, and only parts of Sarah were naked. But, that's another story. Mine is way more exciting than getting your dress stuck on the bleachers and having half of it ripped away."

"Shut up, Parker." Sarah pretended to glare. "At least mine didn't involve a cheerleader and the…"

"Hey, you tell your story and I'll tell mine." Parker teased. "Okay, so senior year in high school. I was eighteen by the way, and this particular story doesn't involve any of the Huskettes."

"As if being underage would have stopped you." Sarah quipped.

Remy watched the banter between the two, an amused look in her eyes. She didn't have that camaraderie with her family. The last of four by ten years, she had come along well after the others had grown up, and they didn't want anything to do with a younger sister. Most of her friends growing up had been acquired in school or on the street. She envied their closeness. She tried to focus on Parker and her tale.

"I was the equipment manager for our softball team. I traveled with the team to all the away games, as well as the coaches and a couple parents. We had a new assistant coach my senior year. Played at Florida State. Great coach, and hot to boot."

Carmen shook her head. "Why do I get the feeling you did something you shouldn't have?"

"Because you know me." Parker squeezed her arm and continued her story.

"Me and a couple of the girls on the team spent most of the season flirting like crazy with her, and aside from a smile here and there, she didn't give us the time of day. Apparently, she had a girl back at Florida State. Anyway, we were getting ready for the last game of semi—state and tensions were running high. We were in second place and one win away from moving on to state."

"Sure it wasn't all the pent up sexual frustration of a bunch of young lezzies in heat?"

"You would think so, at least coming from me. As the equipment manager, it was my responsibility to make sure all the gear was packed on the bus and ready to go. I had finished up and was headed out for the night when I heard someone crying. It was coming from the coach's office. So, I figured I'd better check it out. It was our assistant coach."

"Oh yeah, the old damsel in distress act." Remy teased. "I've seen that one before."

"She was good, had me hook, line and sinker. Apparently, her girl had just told her she had been dating someone else since she left and wanted to end things. I offered my shoulder to cry on."

"And, when she says shoulder, she means face and by cry, she means sit on." Sarah said sarcastically.

Parker looked at her askance. "Whose story is this?"

"Okay, fine, I'll let you tell it."

"Where was I? Oh yes, we were in the middle of a, umm, therapy session and I was knuckle—deep in her snatch when guess who walks in?" She didn't wait for answers. "Yep, the coach. I had her pants down around her ankles and I was licking her like an everlasting gobstopper that had just changed to dessert flavor. I was mortified. She got fired and I got suspended. Fortunately, they couldn't press charges because I wasn't underage. And, that is the most embarrassing thing that has ever happened to me."

Remy and Carmen burst out laughing. "Are you serious? I shouldn't be surprised. We should have known that a girl who, ahh, carries her own *tool belt* would have been trouble in school."

Carmen waggled her finger at Remy. "Still not as embarrassing as Kerry."

Remy groaned loudly. "Man, I had almost forgotten about that."

"Kerry?" Sarah sat up and furrowed her brow at Remy. "What's the Kerry story?"

"Thanks, C." Remy wiped her mouth and threw her napkin at Carmen. "I have to preface this story by saying I am not the greatest speller in the world and there might have been mass quantities of alcohol involved."

"Because you're a lush." Carmen said sarcastically.

"Correction." Remy waggled her eyebrows. "Used to be a lush. Let me set the story up properly. I had been working as an EMT for a couple of years which made it winter of 2002. That's actually where I met C. She was working as a paramedic for the same outfit. Anyway, we had all gone out for our annual Christmas party. My boss's wife was there and she and I had flirted harmlessly since I started there. We were all sitting around the table and my boss goes to the bathroom, mind you leaving his jacket on his chair. I don't know if you know a whole lot about the job, but things were pretty stressful and in our down time, we liked to play practical jokes on each other."

Sarah shook her head. "That doesn't surprise me in the least. Especially, the flirting with the boss's wife part."

Remy shrugged. "Hey, I was young. So, anyway, I see his coat there, and I figure why not check his pockets. Might be something I can use against him later. Lo and behold, I found his cell phone."

"And, she wasn't about to let that opportunity pass."

Remy smirked at Carmen. "No, I didn't. We learned really fast with Jack that we had to get him when we could. So, I figure I'm going to mess with him and Kerry a little bit. I started texting her. All kinds of dirty shit. What I'm going to do to her, maybe sneak into the restroom and fuck her in the stall. I keep sending these texts, and I'm waiting for a reaction and nothing. She doesn't blink, doesn't do anything. So, finally I ask her if she was getting any texts and she says no."

"That should have been your first clue something was up." Carmen snickered.

"Should have been, but I figured that maybe the reception was bad and she just hasn't gotten them yet. I sent one final text and told her to meet me by the restrooms for a quickie. I got up and headed back there, figuring she'd get them all at once and when she came back there, I would tell her it was me messing with her."

"Oh lord, you sent them to someone else, didn't you?" Sarah's shoulders were shaking already, unable to contain her laughter.

"Oh, not just someone else, Jack's brother Cary. Spelled C—A—R—Y, instead of K—E—R—R—Y. I was mortified. For weeks after, they would print out random texts that I'd sent and tape them around work. It was months before I lived that down." Remy's face was bright red, reliving the embarrassment.

When Sarah and Parker finally stopped laughing, Parker shot her a look. "At least, I only got caught with my finger in the pie. Dude, you hit on your boss's brother."

"God, don't remind me. I couldn't face either one of them. On the plus side, Kerry with a K thought it was pretty hot and let's just say most of the texts really happened."

"Shut the fuck up!" Parker leaned forward. "No shit?"

"No shit." Remy smiled. "But, like I said, I was young. I'm not that person anymore." Her eyes found Sarah's, and she could tell by the look on her face, she didn't believe that.

"So, speaking of finger in the pie, are we about done?" Carmen shot Parker a look that let her know she was ready to go.

Parker just grinned like an idiot when Sarah rolled her eyes in her direction.

Remy put her hand on Sarah's arm and smiled. "So, your place or mine?"

Sarah just shook her head. "Mine, I guess, but you're supplying the wine."

Chapter 14

Sarah opened the door and laughed when a bottle of Reisling and a hand snaked around the door. "My favorite!"

Remy gave her a lop—sided grin. "I seem to remember that."

Sarah blushed. It had been a couple of bottles of Reisling that had caused her to lose her inhibitions that night eight years ago. She glared at Remy suspiciously. "Maybe I should stick with water."

"Suit yourself." Remy flopped on the bed. "I'm too tired to try anything tonight anyway."

Sarah immediately smiled. "Okay, fine. I'd hate to let perfectly good wine go to waste. Pour me a glass?"

"Sure." Remy pulled a corkscrew out of her pocket and popped the cork out. "So, tonight's conversation was a little surprising."

"Tell me about it." Sarah took the glass Remy held out to her and sat down on the bed. "That definitely qualifies as more information than I needed to know about my cousin."

Remy laughed. "True. And, I could have lived the rest of my life not knowing that about C."

Sarah was quiet for several moments. "Do women really do that?"

"Do what?" Remy was confused until she saw Sarah's face. "Oh, that. Well, yeah, I guess. I mean I have once or twice."

"And, you liked it?"

"Doing it, yeah." Remy confessed with a smile. "It's kind of a power thing for the one that is, umm, you know wearing it. I haven't ever been on the receiving end, but I assumed from the reaction that it was well—received."

"Hmm, interesting." Sarah fidgeted with her glass. "I just never thought about lesbians using one of those things since we, you know, like women and not guys."

"It's okay to say strap—on, Bonneville. It's not like it's going to jump out of someone's pants and slap you across the mouth."

Sarah snorted. "God, you are silly. Of course I know I can say str…strap—on."

Remy laughed out loud. "Lord, you can barely even get it out of your mouth."

"Strap—on. There, are you happy?" Sarah narrowed her eyes. She reached over and poured herself another glass. She held the bottle out to Remy, who shook her head no, gesturing to her half—full bottle. "Lightweight."

"Maybe." Remy shrugged. "Just exhausted."

Sarah leaned back against the bed and stared at the ceiling, not saying anything for several moments. "Why?"

"Why what?"

"Why do women like it?" Sarah was intrigued by the idea of it and her mind went back to Remy's whispered offer to show her just how much pleasure could be had.

"Hmm, well, wow. Maybe you should lay off the wine." Remy suggested. She didn't mind talking about this, but with Sarah it was impossible to do so without getting even more worked up then she already was. Carmen was just down the hall, getting her brains fucked out and enjoying it, and she was playing the friend card with Sarah.

Remy rubbed the back of her neck, suddenly uncomfortable. She saw Sarah's eyes pleading with her and she swallowed the last of her wine, stealing her frayed nerves. "It feels good."

"Better than, you know, the normal stuff?" The normal stuff was exactly what she and Remy had done over and over again. But, she couldn't bring herself to say it out loud. Oh, but she could think about it, everyday lately. Every night too, which made for some uncomfortable mornings when she couldn't do anything to assuage her arousal.

"Different. It feels good and different." Remy tilted her head. She could tell from the glassy look in Sarah's eyes that her mind was wandering too. She shifted on the bed, trying to release the pressure on her clit to no avail. She could feel it pulsating wildly. "It's just another layer. It adds a little something extra. There's just something about being inside a woman that way. I think that was the only thing I ever envied in a man. Now, I don't have to."

"Wow." Sarah said half to herself. "I never knew."

"Never watched lesbo porn, eh?" Remy smirked. "That'll make a strap—on look tame." Strap—ons, and now porn, and Sarah looking entirely too inviting was more than she should have to bear.

"I guess I haven't lived much at all." Sarah confessed with a rueful smile. "I may have been close to a big town, but growing up we didn't go into the city much. Hell, even college was a small state school."

"There's a whole world out there, Bonneville. You should get out more." Remy thought she would be the perfect person to introduce her to the wilder side of lesbian sex. Unfortunately, in the foreseeable future that didn't seem like an option.

Sarah rolled her eyes. "Oh yeah? In all my spare time?"

"Pay—per view, it's a wonderful invention." Remy forced herself to breathe evenly, not wanting Sarah to know how incredibly worked up she was from a conversation alone.

Sarah snorted. "I don't know about you. But watching porno flicks with my cousin isn't exactly something I aspire too. Besides at four ninety—nine a pop, the bankroll doesn't exactly support that."

"True." Remy divided the last of the wine between Sarah's glass and hers. "Speaking of? Who are you working for now?"

"It's a bit of a secret." Sarah smiled cryptically. She was secretly thankful Remy had steered the conversation back to safer waters. She wasn't sure how much more of that conversation she would stand before she turned her back on common sense and threw herself at Remy. "But, you are the only one I could tell that would appreciate it."

"Oh, this sounds good." Remy leaned forward, intrigued. "Who's your sugar mama?"

"*Rogue Weather.*" Sarah said proudly.

"The TV show?" Remy eyes were wide with disbelief. "That's who you're working for."

"Yep. Pretty sweet gig, huh?"

Remy could only shake her head. "You gotta be shitting me. I've been trying to get them to hire me for a couple years now. How did you score that?"

"Oh God. I shouldn't be telling you this." Sarah winced and shot Remy an apologetic smile. "They contacted me."

Remy groaned loudly. "No fucking way."

"Yeah. I'm sorry." Sarah suddenly wished she could take it back. She hadn't known that Remy had been trying to get her foot in the door with them all this time, and she certainly didn't mean to hurt her feelings. Honestly, had it not been for meeting Remy all those years ago, she would never have had the opportunity. "After word got out that we got film from inside the tornado, they contacted me. They are funding this season, and if it goes well, the next five. All I have to do is keep chasing, and of course, document everything. The footage is exclusively theirs."

"Wow." Remy shook her head several times, still having a hard time comprehending what Sarah was telling her. She was working for the same TV station in Kansas City that she'd started with years ago. The pay was not great, but at least she had funding for what she considered her life's calling. "Well, I can't say I'm not jealous, but that's awesome for you. I'm proud of you, Bonneville. You hit the big time."

"Thanks." Sarah smiled ruefully. "Sometimes, I think it may be too much, though. Now, if I have a bad season, it's not just me I'm letting down, it's a whole group of producers and their executives. I'm just a small fish in a big pond."

"So, why'd you do it?" Remy asked softly. "Why not stay freelance?"

"Honestly? I had too." Sarah ran her hands through her hair. "When Evan left, I didn't have the money to do it anymore. I needed them as much as they thought they needed me. At the time, it was my only option besides going back home and getting a real job."

"Ahh, Evan. That answers a lot." Remy swung her feet up on the bed and leaned back against the headboard. "Never knew what you saw in her."

Sarah laughed. "Tell me how you really feel."

"Maybe I better not. I'd rather you not kick me out just yet. My room isn't ready yet, and the hallway is a bit uncomfortable."

"Okay, fine, you didn't like Evan. What did I see in her?" Sarah tapped her lips with her forefinger. "Now, I'm not sure. At the time, I thought we had a lot in common. She was in the same field, liked a lot of the same things, I was attracted to her. Nothing amazing, but it was good, I guess."

"Good's okay, I suppose." Remy said quietly. She hadn't liked Evan. She knew her from her time chasing, and prior to Sarah, her reputation had preceded her. She played the field with no regard to any of the other players. And, she knew for a fact, if she was in a relationship, it hadn't kept her from sleeping around. That was the one rule Remy had lived by, she didn't cheat. "So, what happened with her?"

Sarah looked at her askance. "Like you don't know?"

"I can speculate." Remy smiled ruefully. "I'm sorry, Bonneville. You deserve better."

"Thanks. I think so too. If she hadn't have left me, I would have broken it off anyway. Especially when I found out she'd been sleeping around pretty much the entire time we were together. I'm a bit naïve, and I guess she figured she could get away with it and I would be none the wiser."

"Naïve or not, you didn't deserve that." Remy's voice was hard, the edge unmistakable. She didn't agree with Evan cheating on anyone, but especially on Sarah. They had never dated, but she felt protective of her nonetheless. It may have been one night to Sarah, but to Remy, it was a night that set off a series of events that changed the course of her life. It was the point in her space—time continuum that had altered her intended course and set her off on a totally different path that had traveled in a parallel line with its mate.

Now, she only had the hard job of convincing Sarah that they had met for a reason and fate had kept them together for a reason. Easier said than done, she was finding out. "I guess the TV gig came at a pretty good time."

"It did. Thankfully, I was able to replace Evan pretty quickly."

"And, thankfully for C, you hired the future love of her life."

Sarah laughed softly. "Crazy, isn't it? How things work out? That they just happened to end up meeting through us."

"Very." Remy turned on her side and propped her head on her hand. "What about us?"

"What do you mean?" Sarah quirked an eyebrow. "What about us?"

"I just think that we keep running into each other for a reason. Someone is trying to tell us something."

"Yeah, that someone is telling us all the tornadoes usually fall in the same place." Sarah laughed. "It's a coincidence, Remy."

"Is it?" Remy voiced her disbelief. "You haven't ever wondered why our lives are so intertwined? That maybe our lives keep overlapping because we are meant for more than just a fling."

Sarah shook her head. She didn't want to admit she had thought about that. There were lots of chasers and yet, Remy was always the one she ran into. It seemed too preordained to be merely chance, but she wouldn't admit that to Remy or to herself. Admitting that, meant admitting that she had also thought, if only briefly, that theirs was a story not yet finished. Maybe one day she would allow herself to feel that, but not today. "We're just lucky, I guess. That, and we are two of the best chasers around. It stands to reason that knowing the weather and following our gut would put us in the same place more often."

"Hmph." Remy snorted in disbelief. "Why is it so hard for you to let me in? I'm not that girl from eight years ago, Sarah." She chose to say Sarah's name, hoping that she would understand she was serious and not just trying to get back in her pants. "I'm not going to hurt you."

Sarah paled. Wasn't that what was really bothering her? Hadn't that been the issue all along? Evan had used her, taken what she wanted and given nothing in return. And, when she was done, she walked away, not caring about the mess she left behind. It had nothing to do with misplaced pride and Sarah's solemn vow not to repeat mistakes of yester years. "It's not that easy, Remy. I know you think it should be, that I'm over complicating things. I won't deny that I am attracted to you. Probably more so than I was eight years ago. I'll admit I do feel something for you, how could I not? That night may have seemed like nothing, but it meant everything. But, I've grown since then and I'll be damned if I'm going to repeat the same mistakes I did. I don't know what you're looking for, but it isn't me. I'm not that woman."

Remy sighed loudly. "So, that's it, end of discussion, just like that?"

"I'm afraid it has to be." Sarah's face was set in determination, but her eyes waivered. The eyes always gave her away. That was the one thing Remy could always count on to gauge her feelings.

Remy swallowed the lump in her throat. No matter what Sarah's eyes were telling her, she still wasn't going to get out of her own way long enough to realize they could have a great future together. She rolled herself off the bed and stretched her body out, yawning loudly.

Sarah's eyes were glued to Remy. Her shirt had come untucked and her abs rippled with every move. Her gaze never left the smooth skin peeking out at her. Her eyes traveled further up, drinking in her small, round breasts, perfectly outlined by her tight tee—shirt. Sarah gulped and licked her lips unaware that Remy was transfixed by the look on her face. A look certainly reserved for a lover, but nakedly displayed on Sarah's face for the world to see.

Remy glanced at her watch, toying with the idea of calling Sarah out. A person just couldn't look at her like that and not expect to be ravaged. "I think I'm going to kick your cousin out. I'm beat."

Sarah nodded quietly. "Probably a good idea." She stood up, stopping next to Remy. "Listen, are you okay with this? I mean, you're fine with us just being…"

Remy silenced her with a look. "No, I'm not, but you haven't given me much choice."

Sarah couldn't move. Remy's gaze rooted her to the floor. She was captivated and lost in Remy's eyes. "Why?"

"Why what?" Remy stepped closer, her body brushing Sarah's.

"Why can't you just let me go?"

"Because of this." Remy wrapped her hand around Sarah's neck and pulled her face to hers. She brushed her lips over Sarah's before she could pull away. She lingered in her softness, tasting the Reisling on her tongue.

Sarah closed the space between them, melding her body with Remy's, their curves fitting together perfectly. Her body was no longer hers to command. In this second, she belonged to Remy. Her tongue tangled with Remy's, eliciting currents of excitement that pooled in her center. All the nights of waking up aroused fueled her hunger. She pushed her doubts to the back of her mind and gave herself to Remy.

Remy groaned as waves of pleasure nipped at her subconscious. Her mouth fit perfectly over Sarah's and kissing her was magical. Her tongue danced inside her mouth and her body ached to touch her. Pulling on every bit of strength she had, she broke the kiss and rested her forehead on Sarah's.

Their breaths were ragged, their pulses hammering wildly. When she could finally breathe again, she rubbed her knuckles over Sarah's cheek. "Why?"

"Why what?" Sarah whispered, trying to keep her knees from buckling.

"Why can't I make you love me?" Remy's voice was ragged with desperation and hunger. She pushed Sarah away gently and smiled. "Good night, Bonneville."

It would be so easy to love you, if only I could let myself. Sarah watched Remy leave, wishing she could find the strength to beg her to stay. She pressed her fingers to her swollen lips and hoped fate knew what she was doing, because she sure as hell didn't.

Chapter 15

Sarah rubbed her eyes tiredly. She hadn't slept well last night. She had only managed to fall into fits of restless sleep, haunted by memories of Remy and their kiss. She took the cup of coffee Parker handed her, ignoring her smirk.

Not letting it slide, Parker nudged her shoulder, almost tipping the cup out of her hand. "Oh shit, I'm sorry, Cuz. So, another sleepless night, huh?"

"I'm sorry. I didn't mean to keep you up." Her brow furrowed. "Wait a minute. No, I'm not sorry. It's because of your little ass I can't sleep."

Parker took a step back, confused. "How's it my fault?"

"If you weren't off gallivanting around with Carmen all night, Remy would not be in my room, and she certainly wouldn't have kissed me last night." Sarah slapped her hand over her mouth. Just as soon as the words tumbled out of her mouth, she wished she could take them back. "I mean, well, can we rewind that?"

"Oh, hell no!" Parker yelled excitedly. "There are no take backs. So, my Cuz actually isn't asexual. I knew something was going on with you two. Now dish."

"First of all, *nothing* is going on. It was just a kiss. Second, of course, I'm not asexual, I'm related to you. How could that even be remotely possible?"

Parker snickered. "Okay, okay. I know, you're all Ms. Sexy Thang, shaking your sexy booty."

Sarah pretended to smack Parker's arm. "Okay, now you're just mocking me."

"Maybe a little." Parker's eyes twinkled mischievously. "Back to the business at hand. *First of all,* a kiss is *never* just a kiss. Believe me. And, second of all, you have got to tell me everything. Do not leave a sister in the dark."

Sarah chuckled, obviously amused with Parker's attempt to be funny. "Fine. We hung out, she kissed me. There's nothing exciting to tell."

"Ooooh, girl." Parker drawled. "Why are you lying to me? Your ears are red, you lying sack of shit. We have a long damn drive today, and you, my dear Cuz, are going to tell me everything."

Sarah sighed. Remy was right, she didn't tell her personal life to anyone, Parker included. She just wasn't one for sharing her feelings and getting all mushy. All her life, she'd been raised with the idea that you didn't cry and you sure as hell didn't talk about shit, except hunting and football. Even when her brother died, no one talked about it. No one grieved publicly. *God, I really do have a fucked up family.*

"I'm waiting." Parker drummed her fingers on the console impatiently. She glanced at her watch and tapped it to make sure it was still working. When she spoke again, there was no mistaking the sarcasm. "Yep, still waiting."

"God, do you ever quit?" Sarah asked with a laugh.

Parker smirked lasciviously. "Fortunately, for Carmen, I don't. I'm like the Energizer bunny. I take a licking and keep on ticking."

Sarah rolled her eyes and shook her head. "That is just like you to make a joke about a pink rabbit with vibrating ears."

Parker snorted out loud. "Oh no, you didn't just make a joke about a vibrator?"

"See, I know about toys." Sarah said smugly. "I did go to college. You didn't actually think the only thing I ever did was study, did you?"

"Mmm, mmm, mmm. I'll be damned." Parker slapped her knee. "Guess there is more to my little Cuz than I gave you credit for. I'm guessing that means there might be more to the Remy story than you are divulging."

Sarah blushed and held up her thumb and forefinger. "Maybe a little bit."

"Oh, I knew it!" Parker exclaimed. She turned in the seat and faced Sarah. "Out with it."

"Okay, when you asked how Remy and I knew each other, I may not have been entirely forthcoming."

"No shit, Sherlock. Didn't take a genius to figure that one out."

"We met about eight years ago, right after the Stockton tornado. I was working as a meteorologist, covering a line of storms in Kansas that Remy had followed. I fell in love..." Sarah glared at Parker. "Don't oooh me. I didn't fall in love with her, I fell in love with chasing after hearing her talk about it. I also fell for her lines that night. We ended up sleeping together."

"Oh fuck. That is juicier than I thought. I figured you for a hot and heavy make out session, but you slept with her. No fucking way!"

"Yes, Sarah has had sex." Sarah sounded like a robot, teasing Parker.

"So, was it good?"

Sarah's face reddened and she felt her chest tighten. "This is very hard to admit to, but yes, it was fan—fucking—tastic. I haven't been with anyone since then who has made me feel like Remy does."

Parker grinned wickedly. "So, let me guess, Remy hasn't forgotten either, and she's spent the last eight years trying to rekindle the fire."

"Yes." Sarah admitted quietly. "And, she surprised me with the kiss last night."

"So, what's the big deal? You hooked up once, what's stopping you now?"

Sarah shrugged. "I spent the last eight years replaying that night in my head with the hopes of reminding myself never to make the same mistake again."

"Why is it a mistake? Remy's a great girl. You could do a lot worse."

"I know. I just can't open myself up and…"

"Get hurt again." Parker finished her sentence. "So what, you're going to be a storm chasing nun for the rest of your life?"

"Funny." Sarah looked at Parker askance. "No, I'm not going to take a vow of celibacy and be a nun, but I'm also not going to sleep with Remy again."

"Why the hell not?" Parker asked incredulously. "Especially, if it's the best fuck you ever had."

"God, could you be any more crude?"

Parker waggled her eyebrows. "Don't tempt me. I just don't get it. I mean you say she's the best *relations* you ever had. She obviously wants you, and I've seen the way she looks at you when she thinks no one is looking. She's halfway in love with you already."

"Don't say that. That only makes it worse."

"How?"

"Don't you see, it's always worse when emotions get involved. Look at us, eight years later, and neither one of us has been able to let go. Giving in to our attraction will only lead to heartache."

"I'm confused." Parker furrowed her brow. "I don't understand why you think you're going to get hurt."

"I know Remy, and I know her reputation. I ignored Evan's past and look where it got me."

"Fuck Evan." Parker spat out. "I never saw her look at you the way Remy does."

"Can we just let it go?" Sarah pleaded softly. "This is why I don't talk about stuff with you, or anyone else for that matter. I hate talking about my feelings."

"Fine, whatever." Parker shook her head. "I guess if you want to let your shit grow back together from non—use, that's your prerogative."

"There is seriously something wrong with you." Sarah rolled her eyes at her cousin. Her comments shouldn't surprise her. Parker could be incredibly inappropriate and had spent a lot of time in detention growing up. It wasn't any different twenty years later.

"You have no idea." Parker smirked. "You should have heard me last night…"

"La, la, la." Sarah took her hands off the wheel and put her fingers in her ears. "I can't hear you."

Parker busted out laughing. "Oh yeah, better not tell you anything to tempt you out of your life of celibacy."

Sarah smacked her arm. "Shut up. I am not celibate." *Or am I?* Now that she thought about it, she kind of was. She hadn't been with anyone since Evan, and that hadn't been very often.

"Mmm—hmmm. You just keep telling yourself that." Parker pretended to study the radar on her phone all the while humming "Celibacy Blues" by Rascal Flatts.

"I know what you're doing."

"What?" Parker shrugged innocently, but her eyes twinkled mischievously. "Is it working?"

"No." Sarah tried to stop the corners of her mouth from creeping up. "Maybe."

"I'll settle for a maybe." She flashed the phone at Sarah. "So, where we headed to boss?"

"Really?" Sarah tried to be stern, but she couldn't help laughing at Parker. "Alabama. There's something brewing down there. Could get crazy."

"Nothing on the radar right now." Parker countered.

"Yeah, but there is an upper—level trough moving across the Southern Plains and a mid—level jet stream moving in from the north. If that jet stream gets in behind the trough, we may be in for what us meteorologists like to call the perfect storm. For us, it's a once in a lifetime thing."

Parker's face turned several shades paler. "Worse than Oklahoma?"

Sarah could hear the concern in her voice and her heart went out to her. "I'm sorry Parker. I should never have asked you to do this."

"No, no. It's okay. Beats *'What can the brown do for you?'"* Parker said sarcastically, referring to her job driving for UPS. "Although, I did get a lot of pussy doing that job."

Sarah groaned loudly. "Is that all you think about?"

"Pretty much." Parker smiled smugly. "Now, if they had a job doing that, I would be so money."

"Seriously, do you listen to yourself?"

"Well, no, I never thought about taping myself having sex." Parker waggled her eyebrows. "Just kidding. I can't help. It is all I think about. It's sooo good. I pretty much worship women. I am probably a guy trapped in a lesbian's body."

"You're probably a lesbian trapped in a man's mind stuck in a lesbian's body."

"Yeah, that's probably closer to the truth." Parker chuckled. "Admitting I have a problem is the first step towards recovery."

"Uh—uh, I don't think there's any hope for you. You're a functioning sex—aholic. I've just got to accept it."

Parker snorted. "I'm trying. At least, I'm limiting it to one woman lately. And, I'm kind of thinking I might actually be becoming a one—woman lesbian. I'm letting the brown do for me."

"That's so mature of you, Parker." Sarah teased sarcastically. "There might actually be hope for you yet.

Although, I'm pretty sure it's politically incorrect to call Carmen the brown girl."

"Hey, she calls herself that, I don't want to offend."

"Right. Like all of a sudden you care about what people think."

"Let's just say, I'm finally growing up." Parker said proudly, then laughed. "Or, at least I'll say I'm thinking about it."

"Oh God, don't think too hard. I don't want you to get a headache."

"Funny, Sarah." Parker tapped the map. "Why don't you just shut up and drive?"

Chapter 16

Remy drained the last of her Mt. Dew and scanned the horizon. They had passed a couple other chasing teams on the fourteen—hour drive from Iowa to Alabama, but hadn't passed the hail battered Chevy. She knew without speaking to Sarah that she would be heading in the same direction. Both were seasoned chasers, and especially recently, had an uncanny knack for showing up in the same place. Sarah may not have liked it, but it pleased Remy to no end.

"They're already here, Chica." Carmen's amused tone interrupted her thoughts.

"Who's already here?" Remy asked nonchalantly, but Carmen read her like a dime store hooker.

"You know." Carmen smirked, obviously not letting Remy off the hook. "Pretty excited to get there myself."

"I'm sure." Remy said sarcastically. "Picking up where you left off?"

"Well that and…" Carmen's eyes twinkled wickedly. "Got a text from Parker. Apparently, she's got some pretty good gossip to tell me. A little something about Sarah hooking up with someone. You wouldn't happen to know what she was talking about, would you?"

Remy shrugged and shook her head feigning innocence. "Nope, can't say that I do."

"Tu eres tanta." Carmen said with a chuckle. "You think I don't know something is going on with you?"

127

"Did you just call me a fool?" Remy asked incredulously.

"Si, Chica. Because you are a fool. I got eyes, you know? I can see what's going on right in front of me."

Remy rolled her eyes. "There's nothing to see, because there is nothing going on."

"Uh-huh. Just like nothing happened that night you met Sarah."

Remy's face went white. "What do you know about that night?"

"I know you guys disappeared, and I didn't see you till the next morning. You want to try and tell me that you were studying weather charts?" Carmen teased her mercilessly. "I'm just betting that Sarah's little hookup has everything to do with you."

"Nah." Remy shook her head. "Besides, we didn't hook up. It was just a kiss."

"Mierda!" Carmen slapped her thigh. "I knew it! You got the hots for her, huh?"

"Maybe." Remy blushed.

"You better tell me about this kiss, Chica."

"It's not a big deal, C. Just let it go okay?" Remy pleaded with Carmen. "I'm not sure anything will even come of it, but I don't want you two hoo—hahs ruining my chances by ragging on her about it."

Carmen's eyes widened and she put her palms up feigning innocence. "Who, me?"

"Yes, you, Ms. Nosy Pants." Remy smiled.

"If it gets you laid, I'll take a vow of silence."

Remy snorted loudly. "You, not talk? That's the funniest shit I've ever heard."

Carmen glared at Remy and waggled her finger in her face. "Keep it up, Chica. Don't make me go all Puerto Rican on your ass."

"Truce." Remy begged. "The last time you did that it was four straight days of yelling at me in Spanish. Ay, ya, ya, I couldn't take that again."

"You give up too fast, Chica." Carmen scolded mildly. "I hope you have more fight in you for Sarah. She will chew you up and spit you out."

"Hey, if it involves me and her and eating in the same sentence, she can do whatever she wants."

Carmen groaned loudly.

"Hey, if I have to sit and listen to you and Parker and your bad hotdog jokes, you can tolerate my pie jokes."

"I'm just saying that woman is fire. I see the way she glares at you. It's not pretty and if you are going to handle that one, you are going to have to grow some balls."

"Or...I could just borrow Parker's." Remy snickered at Carmen's look of disgust.

"You want to play for her team, you gotta get your own balls, Chica."

"Fine." Remy conceded. "And, don't you worry about me. I can handle her just fine. *If she'll give me a chance.*" Remy added under her breath.

"Que?"

"Nada. Just talking to myself." Remy checked the gauges. "Shit, we gotta get gas. We are way passed empty. See what happens when you get me off track?"

"Dios mio." Carmen exclaimed loudly. "You've been on the left side of the street since we ran into Sarah."

Remy laughed out loud. "You mean out in left field."

"Street, field, whatever. You've been a whole different Remy the past few weeks."

"You don't like it?"

"Nah, I'm not saying that. I'm just saying you are different. More focused on the things going on around you, not the old Remy that was solely focused on just this." Carmen spread her hands out, encompassing the vehicle around them.

Remy knew she was talking about chasing in general. She was right, this had been her life for longer than she could count on one hand. She was still as dedicated as before, she was just starting to realize that there might be room in her life to actually have a life. "I'm growing, what can I say?"

"I like this new you. You're much more fun to be around."

Carmen smiled. She didn't need Remy to acknowledge her existence outside of being her spotter, but it made her feel good knowing that maybe all the years they had shared a tiny space together had made an impression on Remy. Maybe, when they joked about being friends, they really were. And maybe, just maybe, Remy had room in her heart for more than the nameless souls she was trying to save. Maybe she actually had room in her heart for herself.

"Gracias, C. In my old age, I'm realizing that I need more than this to be complete. I'm content with my life, but I see the way you and Parker look at each other, and I know I'm missing out. I kiss Sarah one time, and in that instant, a future very different than the one I planned flashed in front of me, and you know what, I liked it. I want more. I want the whole nine yards. I've locked myself away in Thor for too long. I realize there is room for more than one love in my life." *Now I just have to convince Sarah she wants the same thing.*

"In your *old age*, you have gotten pretty smart." Carmen smiled from ear—to—ear, watching Remy deftly maneuver Thor into a lane at the far end of the gas station. "Think you can still pump the gas, or do you need me to do it, old timer?"

"You're a funny girl." Remy jumped out of the truck and started the pump. She knocked on Carmen's window and when she rolled it down, she smiled ruefully. "I'm gonna grab another pop. You want anything?"

"An extra hot, non—fat, soy latte, light foam, no whip." Carmen laughed at Remy's exaggerated glare. "Kidding. Just grab me some gas station coffee. But you owe me a frou—frou drink from Starbucks."

"Deal." Remy jogged away. Moments later, she deposited a steaming cup of coffee in Carmen's hands. Remy had already drained half of one soda and had a second tucked under her arm. She caught Carmen's sideways glance and shrugged her shoulders. "What? I'm tired."

"Uh—huh."

Carmen scanned the radar while Remy topped the tank off and got back in the truck with a sigh.

"Is it close?"

"Another couple of hours, I think." She held the phone up for Remy to see. "But, there is definite movement in this storm. This one's big, Rem. Biggest of the season.

Remy could only nod. Carmen hadn't exaggerated. The jet stream had caught up with the trough they had been watching, and the radar flashed way more red than green.

"Where should we camp out?"

Remy rubbed her chin thoughtfully. "I'm thinking anywhere in this corridor." She pointed at a strip between Mississippi and Alabama. "This storm's already dropped funnels in Oklahoma and Texas. I think that was just the beginning. I say we hang out somewhere south of Tuscaloosa."

Carmen nodded. "I don't even know where to begin. There's massive supercells everwhere."

"I'm watching this cell." Remy pointed at a large cell centered about fifty miles north of Jackson, Missisippi. "This one just looks bad."

"Alright, let's do it then."

Remy pointed the truck back out on the highway. The system they were watching was part of a major system that covered half the US. It had already kicked several tornadoes out, one measuring an EF4. It had leveled the small town of Cullman. The other thing that worried Remy more than anything were reports that the storms had knocked out power for most of the residents in the storm's path, making it nearly impossible to issue warnings. If more tornadoes did touch down, she could only pray that everyone had made it to safety.

They had made good time so far, but when they hit rain just outside of Fayette, they slowed considerably. "Shit, this is nuts." Remy squinted, trying to make out the road through the water pouring down the windshield. "I hope it doesn't stay this bad."

"Shouldn't." Carmen said after looking at the radar. "We should drive out of this in a couple of minutes."

Remy's phone buzzed crazily on the console. She tossed it to Carmen. "Text. Check it."

"Dios mio." Carmen said as she read the text. "It's Sarah. There's a tornado down in Lawrence County. They are following it now."

"Tell her to be careful and try not to be a hero." Remy shook her head. "Oh shit, that means Parker is driving. Is she crazy?"

Carmen swallowed a lump in her throat. This was Parker's first season. She shouldn't be driving, at least not in the middle of a chase. "Why isn't Sarah driving?"

"My guess, she didn't want to miss any of the footage."

"Again…is she crazy?"

"Probably a little. Hopefully, she doesn't have Parker trying anything crazy." Remy prayed they were all right. It was one thing to drive into a tornado with Thor. It was entirely different, and potentially suicidal, to do so in Sarah's car. She silently cursed Sarah's contract with *Rogue Weather*. Hopefully, her need for funding wouldn't outweigh common sense. "I'm sure they are fine."

Remy passed a small sign announcing Tuscaloosa in twenty miles. She grabbed the map and flicked her eyes between that and the road. "I'm going to come around on Highway 11."

Twenty minutes later, she parked on the shoulder. One glance at the sky, and Remy knew this storm was a bad one. "These trees are killing us. We need to get to a clearing."

She drove and kept a massive supercell in her rear view mirror.

"Park here." Carmen pointed to a break in the trees where they could see farmland for several miles. "This is good." She pointed at a large hook echo in the supercell just behind them. "Look at the rotation in this cell. It's churning."

Remy grabbed her camera and got out, shooting several shots of the wall cloud that arched above them. "There, there. We've got a tail. It's coming down. Oh God, C, it's massive."

Carmen pointed out in the field. "Debris, we've got debris. That funnel is down."

"It's gotta be moving a good fifty, sixty miles an hour." Remy continued snapping pictures. "Oh shit, oh shit! Power lines, it's snapping the power lines." She saw the telltale spark of electricity as the tornado shredded across the fields, ripping up power lines.

"Rem, we gotta move! It's shifting, it's shifting!" Carmen was waving excitedly. "Rem, get us out of here!"

Remy turned on the engine and gunned it. The tires whined in protest. They couldn't get traction on the wet pavement. She watched the massive tornado coming straight for them. It was at least three—quarters of a mile wide and bearing down on them faster than they could move.

"Come on. Get this fucking thing moving!" Carmen shouted above the massive roar behind them. "Let's go!"

"I'm trying." Remy let off the gas, letting the tires grip and then she gunned it. She could see trees in her mirror being ripped up and flung out in the road. The last thing she wanted was a huge branch coming at her face. Her hands were ghostly white where she gripped the steering wheel and she could hear Carmen praying in Spanish.

Even though they had ridden one tornado in Thor and survived, this tornado would shred them to pieces. Remy guessed it to be an EF4, one of the strongest tornadoes possible. She couldn't tell which was louder, her heart beating or the massive rush of wind that sounded like a freight train running through her head.

"Faster, you have to go faster!" Carmen shouted.

"I'm trying. Don't you think I know that?" Remy yelled, her fear making her edgy. She passed cars on the highway and she waved her hand at the drivers to turn around. "Tornado! Turn around! Turn around! Can't they see a fucking tornado about to take them out?"

She could hear Thor's engine protesting her demands to speed up. "God, come on!" Her heart raced and beads of sweat rolled down her face. Just when she thought she wouldn't out run it, the tornado shifted directions and headed north again. She pulled over and got out of the truck. Her body shook all over.

Carmen was laughing nervously. "Oh man, that was close. I can't believe we made it."

They watched the tornado in awed silence. It hadn't gotten smaller, in fact it looked like it had grown in size. They had seen hundreds of tornadoes over the years but this one was unlike any other. Remy guessed it had already cut a path over twenty miles long, making it one of the longest tornado paths on record.

"Rem?" Carmen nudged her arm lightly.

"Yeah."

"It's heading straight for Tuscaloosa. If it stays together, they are screwed."

"Oh shit." Remy looked at the bright red rotation on the radar. Tuscaloosa was directly in the line of the storm. "Get in. Whatever happens, they are going to need some help."

Remy gunned the engine, and this time the wheels grabbed and Thor jumped like a jackrabbit out of the gate. There was no way they would beat the storm, she only hoped that after it hit, her training would be of use. Her thoughts flashed back to her days as an EMT. She could still see the blank, hollow eyes staring out at her and the thought made her shiver.

Carmen squeezed her arm. "Maybe it won't be as bad."

Remy shook her head, her eyes grim. "I'm afraid it's going to be worse."

They could still see the massive wedge tornado in the distance and the amount of debris getting pulled into the vortex was unlike anything they had ever seen. Remy's eyes never left the tornado and Carmen had the camera trained on it, recording every detail of the storm as it raged its fury on anything in its path.

"I just hope they saw it coming." Remy's voice shook with unmistakable uncertainty. "Otherwise, there is no telling what we will find."

Aside from the sound of the road, neither one spoke again until they pulled into the city. Nothing could have prepared them for the devastation that awaited them. Tuscaloosa had been leveled. Remy's heart broke again and she struggled with the knowledge that she was no closer to figuring out the violent storms today than she was eight years ago.

Every building for miles had been demolished, cars had been thrown around like toys and trees lay upended as far as she could see. The first people were just coming outside, stunned looks on their faces. She could hear sirens in every direction. She swallowed the massive lump in her throat and let out a heart—wrenching wail. "It's just not fair, it's just not fucking fair."

Carmen squeezed her hand. "Come on. They need us." She was the level—headed one now, her emotions shoved deep inside. If she didn't get Remy's head on straight, she would be no help to anyone, least of all herself. She forced Remy to park the truck.

Remy shook off her doubts, taking several deep breaths to steel herself for the task at hand. She started walking in the direction of the worst damage, praying she found life and not the grim faces of death.

"There!" Carmen shouted, pointing at a man struggling to get his leg out from under a large beam. She squeezed Remy's hand one last time. "You can do this, Chica. This is why we are here."

Remy stumbled over piles of debris on her way to help him. "You alright? You alright?"

"Yeah, just my leg." The man said shakily.

"We'll get you out. What's your name?" A calm serene had overtaken Remy, and the years of training came back to her.

"Peter."

"Peter, good to meet you. Why don't we get this off your leg?" She pulled on the beam unable to budge it. "C, come here. Grab something to wedge this off."

Carmen grabbed a smaller two—by—four and shoved it under the beam. "Just hang on Peter, we'll get you out." She shouted over the sudden barrage of sirens. She glanced over and saw dozens of ambulances and police cars converging on the main road.

They gripped the two—by—four and heaved until they felt it budge. The beam moved with a groan. Remy let go long enough to grab Peter's arm and pull him out. She knelt over him and pulled his pant leg up gingerly. She grimaced when she saw the jagged edge of his tibia poking out of his skin. She hoped her face hadn't paled enough to worry him. "How you doing, Peter? How's the pain?"

He tried to look at his leg but Remy wouldn't let him. "I'm…I'm alright I guess. Can't really feel it right now."

Remy chuckled nervously. "That's probably good for now. The shock is keeping you from feeling the pain. There's a good chance that you broke your leg. I think we need to get it stabilized and see about getting you to the hospital."

She grimaced. More than likely, he wouldn't be seen tonight. Given the devastation around them, his wounds would more than likely be considered minor in a hospital full of people with life—threatening injuries. "Can you hold still for a bit longer? I'm going to try to splint it to prevent any further damage?"

"Yeah, I…I…th…think…s…so." Peter's teeth were chattering. The shock was making him cold and she needed to get him calmed down.

"Hey, Peter, can you take a couple of deep breaths?" She rubbed his arms vigorously trying to get him warm. "Just think about someplace warm, okay?"

Peter managed to shake his head up and down.

Remy found several small pieces of wood and using strips she made out of her sweatshirt, she gently bound his leg, stabilizing it against further movement. "All set, Peter. Think you can hang out here for a bit while I check things out."

Another shake of the head and a small smile and Remy was off. She headed around what would have been the back of the house where she'd seen Carmen head earlier. "C? C? Where are you?"

"Help!"

A chill ran up Remy's spine. She'd heard those pleas before. "Hang on, I'm coming!" She tried to locate the voice. "Where are you?"

"Here! Here!" A muffled voice came from a pile of rubble two houses down.

Remy jumped around debris, following the voice. "Hello?"

"I'm here, please help me."

Remy's eyes searched what was left of the house. She spotted a mattress with a large tree branch lying on top of it. She started climbing over the rubble, throwing pieces of it aside as she made her way to the mound where she'd heard the voice. She bent over and saw a hand reaching out from beneath the tattered fabric. "Hey, hey. I'm here. You okay?"

"I'm okay, but please my daughter's under here and she's not moving. Please help her!"

Remy felt her heart drop. It was happening all over again. Here she was facing death again.

"Please, get us out of here."

Remy gulped. "I'm coming, I'm coming. I'm going to get you out." She eyed the massive branch and knew from the circumference that she wasn't moving it on her own. "C! C! Where are you?" She waited, praying for her to respond.

"Yo, Rem. Over here." Carmen came around a tall pile carrying a small dog, who was huddled against her body. "Whatchu got?"

Remy nodded towards the mattress. "Got at least two in there. Mother and daughter. We have to get them out." She leaned towards Carmen and spoke softly. "Mom says her daughter is not moving."

"Oh shit." Carmen set the puppy down on a patch of bare grass and pushed her sleeves up. "Then we better get the fucking thing off." She looked around, scanning for something to help move the tree. Not seeing anything, she wiped her brow in exasperation.

"Please hurry." The voice pleaded again. "You have to get my daughter out."

Remy shook her head. "We've got to figure something out. We gotta get her out."

She knelt down and peaked under the mattress. "Ma'am, here's the situation. You've got a large tree sitting on top of you. I'm not sure we can get it off without help. What we're going to try to do for now is get your daughter out from under there so we can get her taken care of. We're gonna need your help if you can manage."

"Yes anything. I'll do anything." She said quickly. Her voice was shaking and her breath was coming in loud, ragged gasps.

"Ma'am, my name's Remy and we're gonna get through this. What's your name?" Remy knew she needed to keep her calm if she had any hopes of getting them both out alive. "Christine."

"Christine, what's your daughter's name?"

"Sarah, her name's Sarah."

Remy's heart jumped. She didn't believe in coincidences. Something had brought her here today, and to this exact spot, because she was meant to save this little girl. More resolute now, she was wholly focused on the small little girl who desperately needed her help. "Okay, Christine, we're gonna get Sarah out. She's gonna be okay, I promise. I need you to tell me if you can feel her. Is she close to you?"

"I can feel her hand, that's all." Christine said quickly.

"Okay, that's good. Has she moved since the mattress fell on you?"

"No, no, she hasn't. Please, get her out. She's all I have."

Remy looked at Carmen, fear in her eyes. Carmen nodded at her, silently telling her it would be okay. She would be fine. "Christine, where is she in relation to you?"

"She's by my leg."

Remy slid her arm under the mattress. "Can you touch my hand?"

She felt ice cold fingers graze hers. "Okay, is that your right hand or left?"

"My left."

"Is Sarah on your right or your left?"

"My…my right."

Remy frowned. Sarah's position in relation to Christine's body meant she was under the side of the mattress where the heavier part of the branch rested. She prayed the little girl was all right. She had to be, she had promised her mother she would be okay.

Remy looked up at Carmen. "I need a really strong board, narrow if possible and some smaller, thicker boards that we can wedge underneath it. Ones without sharp edges if possible."

Carmen nodded and started searching the piles around them.

"Okay, Christine, here's what we are going to do." Remy outlined her plan, the entire time praying that it worked.

Carmen started bringing boards back and stacking them at Remy's feet. "'Kay, tell me what to do?"

"I'm going to slide this long one in. Christine, you ready?"

"Yes."

"I'm going to slide the first board in. Christine, I need you to place it as close to Sarah as you can. We'll start using the smaller boards and wedge them under the first one. Hopefully, we will get enough space in there that you can slide Sarah to me." Remy rubbed her hands together nervously. "Everybody ready?"

Christine said yes almost before she asked the question.

"Okay, let's do this." Remy slid the first board under the mattress, meeting resistance almost immediately. She grunted loudly, trying to shove it under, not wanting to hit Christine. "Hey, Christine, can you put your hand on the edge of the board and kind of guide it in?"

"I don't know. My arm's pinned."

"Shit!" Remy swore softly. "This is going to be harder than I thought. C, we're going to have to start wedging the boards under there further out and hope we can slide them under this one enough to lift the mattress up."

Carmen glanced at Remy and pointed at her watch. *"This needs to happen fast. She's been under there at least fifteen minutes.*" Carmen whispered so as not to scare Christine.

Remy nodded. "Okay, Christine. We're going with Plan B. It's going to be a little more uncomfortable for you, but it should work."

"O…okay." Christine's voice shook. "Anything, just please get Sarah out."

Remy pulled the board up and nodded at Carmen. "Start sticking them under here. We'll work our way back to Sarah."

"Si." Carmen pushed the first piece of wood in with a loud grunt.

"That's it, keep them coming." Remy strained against the weight on top of the board. Carmen shoved another piece of wood under the board, followed by three more in succession. She could finally see Christine's arm under the mattress and she felt the first glimmer of hope. "That's it. It's working."

Carmen brought more pieces and shoved them under quickly. "I think it's working, Chica."

"Me too." Remy said excitedly. "Christine, how's it feeling? Can you breathe a little more?"

"Yes, yes, it's better. Hurry!"

Remy's arms shook violently with exhaustion. She'd been holding the board now for what seemed like an eternity. She wasn't sure where the strength was coming from, but she imagined the adrenaline pumping through her veins had something to do with it. She could make out Christine's shoulder now. She saw dried blood caked on her arm and hoped the cuts weren't bad. "How's the pain, Christine?"

"Feels like I got run over by a tornado." Christine said with a nervous chuckle.

Remy smiled, her sense of humor was still intact. That was a good sign. "You should see the other guy, right?"

Remy felt a surge of energy. "Come on, girls. Let's finish this." She peered under the mattress. "Christine, can you move enough to pull Sarah out?"

Christine grunted loudly. "I…I think so."

Remy waited for what seemed like an eternity when she felt a small hand brush hers. "I've got her. I've got her!" She eased the small body out and leaned over her quickly. She grabbed her wrist and felt for a pulse. Finally, she felt a weak tremor and she cried out hysterically. "She's okay, she's okay! She's just unconscious. I can't tell for sure if she's got any broken bones, but she's okay."

"Oh my god, thank you!" Christine whispered quietly.

Remy's eyes covered Sarah's body, looking for signs of bruising or internal bleeding. There was a possibility that Sarah had a concussion and she would need to be checked by a doctor, but otherwise she seemed no worse for wear.

"Hhh-hmmm." Christine wriggled her hand. "Do you think you could get me out? My bladder's about to burst."

Remy laughed out loud. Her fear gave way to relief, and she felt a rush of emotions flood her body. "I think that can be arranged."

It took them another twenty minutes to create a big enough space to pull Christine out. When she wriggled free, she crawled towards Sarah's body and hugged her tightly. "You're okay, baby, we're going to be okay. Mommy's got you now."

She pushed herself off the ground and threw her arms around Remy and Carmen. "Thank you so much. You saved our lives."

Remy blushed. "We were just in the right place at the right time."

"God sent you here. We are forever in your debt."

"Back here!"

Remy turned and saw several first responders rounding what was left of the houses behind them. She squeezed

Christine's arm. "They need to check Sarah out, make sure the concussion isn't serious."

She started to walk away with Carmen when Christine's hand pulled her back. "Thank you, Remy. I'll never forget what you did for us."

Remy smiled and waved, stepping aside as the paramedics swarmed around Christine and her daughter. They were safe now and that was all that mattered.

Chapter 17

Sarah brought the car to a screeching halt on the outskirts of Birmingham. "Shit!" She could see large pieces of debris flying around the base of the massive wedge tornado, now almost two and a half miles wide. It was so massive that unless they stayed several miles away, they wouldn't have even been able to tell it was a tornado.

They had followed this same storm on the radar from before it touched down outside of Tuscaloosa. "There's no way, there's just no way. That thing's been on the ground for over eighty miles. That's impossible."

"Nothing's impossible today. Four EF5 tornadoes already. You said yourself that never happens."

Sarah shook her head at Parker. "It doesn't happen. Maybe one a year. That's it." She kept the camera pointed at the tornado as it cut a large swath into the heart of Birmingham. "God help them."

They had heard other spotters talking about the devastation in Tuscaloosa and it looked as though Birmingham was going to suffer the same fate. The loss of life today would be a sobering reminder to all that humans aren't as invincible as we believe we are. Against massive tornadoes, we are merely playthings. All the more reason, spotters like Sarah and Remy continued to chase. The more information they gathered in the fight against the weather, the more advances would be made towards finding and engineering warning systems that would sound not just minutes before, but maybe hours.

Unlike hurricanes that could be monitored and tracked days in advance, tornadoes gave no indication of when they would drop and the storms around them made them all the more dangerous. Today's massive tornado event was made exponentially more dangerous due to the storms that preceded this round, knocking out power to hundreds of thousands of people and with that, taking away the ability to warn them of the impending danger.

Sarah's hand shook as she kept the camera trained on the tornado as it ripped through the city, shredding trees and buildings with little more effort than blowing grains of sand out of her hand, and with no more regard for life than a stealthy killer. Her breath came in quick gasps, the air punctuated with audible, yet unintelligible words muttered between breaths.

After what seemed an eternity, the winds mellowed to a disconcerting stillness. The thundering roar now a muffled rumble muted by an indeterminable distance. Sarah laid the camera on the seat next to her and rubbed her temples. She was tense and on edge and almost afraid to drive into the city, not sure what awaited them and even more unsure that she was prepared to face it.

She put her hand over Parker's and searched her eyes. "We need to help."

Parker nodded. "I'm ready."

Sarah followed Highway 31 into the city. The tornado had devastated a large strip on the north side of Birmingham. Sarah drove slowly, unable to believe this used to be a neighborhood with homes and buildings. The only things visible now were huge mounds of debris. Cars flipped on top of what were only minutes before homes. Stunned faces walked the littered streets and she could see from the despondent tears that the storm had taken its toll in the worst way possible.

She slowed the car and grabbed her camera. The footage she gathered was for more than her documentary. She filmed as a way for the world to know what this town had suffered. For those on the outside, it would be a visual remembrance of the hurt their brethren had endured, and hopefully foster in them a longing to render aid. Without help, the town would be lost, another victim of a senseless storm. Sarah had seen that too many times and this was her way of bringing the pain to the world outside Birmingham and bringing help from the outside world to Birmingham.

"There!" Parker shouted, pointing at what could only have been a house.

A woman was wandering around with blood streaming from a cut on her forehead. Her eyes were unfocused and Sarah could tell she was in shock. She shut the engine off and jumped out, grabbing a bottle of water and Parker's doo—rag. "Ma'am? Ma'am?"

Her voice never even phased the woman. She wandered aimlessly, stumbling over pieces of debris in the yard. Sarah touched her arm softly, not wanting to startle her. "Ma'am?"

The woman finally turned and her unseeing eyes slowly focused on Sarah's face. "Yes?"

"Are you okay?" Sarah guided her to the edge of the yard and helped her sit down on the sidewalk. "Your head? It's cut pretty bad."

The woman looked at her, confusion in her eyes. "What?"

"Your head is bleeding. Let me help you get it cleaned up."

"Oh alright, dear." Her voice shook softly.

Sarah soaked the doo—rag and gently dabbed the area around the cut. She used the opportunity to study the woman's face. Her eyes were crystal blue surrounded by years of laugh lines. Gray hair framed an oval face and somewhere in her storied past, she'd gotten a scar that ran the length of her left cheek. Sarah shook her head, knowing the large gash on her forehead would be yet another scar.

"I'm sorry if I hurt you." Sarah said softly, searching the woman's face for signs of pain.

"What dear?" The woman blinked and her eyes settled on the wet rag. "Oh no, dear, I'm fine."

She wasn't fine, but Sarah didn't see any reason to dispute her statement. "I'm going to leave you here for a few minutes." She nodded towards the pile behind them. "Is this your house behind us?"

The woman glanced over her shoulder. "Oh yes, dear. That's mine and Charlie's house. That's my husband, Charlie."

"Charlie?" Sarah's brow furrowed. "Where's Charlie now? Is he still alive?"

"Oh my heavens, no. Charlie's been gone almost ten years now." A look of sadness flashed across her face and then her mouth smiled. "Charlie built our house with his own hands. He was wonderful."

"Mom! Mom!"

Sarah looked up and saw a middle—aged woman running towards them.

"Mom! Are you okay?"

"Oh yes, honey. I'm fine." She patted Sarah's hand. "This young lady took good care of me."

The newcomer knelt down in front of her mother and surveyed her face. Somewhat appeased by her mother's calm demeanor, she stood and smiled at Sarah. "Thank you."

Sarah put her hand up, dismissing the thank you. "It was nothing. I'm just glad you're here to get her out of this mess."

The woman nodded, her eyes silently telegraphing her thanks. She helped her mother off the curb and slipped her arm through her mother's. Sarah watched them until the car drove around a corner, thankful that she was okay and even more thankful that this stranger whom she'd never met, had survived the tragedy.

"Sarah." Parker's voice broke through her ruminations. "Sarah, come over here quick."

She turned and followed the voice, skidding to a stop next to Parker. Her eyes followed Parker's finger and she gasped out loud when she saw an arm peeking out from underneath a large piece of wood. She immediately started pulling pieces of wood and metal away from the body.

When she finally uncovered the body, she felt her stomach roil violently. His face was pale and his skin had taken on the gray palour of death. Sarah's mind went back fifteen years and she saw her brother lying there, his life ebbing away.

"Is he…" Parker's voice cracked, and she put her hand over her mouth willing the contents of her stomach back down.

"I don't know." Sarah kneeled beside him and felt his neck for a pulse. "Oh my God!"

"Oh shit." Parker breath stuck in her throat.

"No, no. Maybe it's not too late." Sarah ran her fingers along his stomach until she located his zyphoid process at the bottom of his sternum. She put the heel of her hand just above her fingers, and interlocked her right hand on top of her left hand. "I'm going to need your help."

Parker's face paled even more. "I can't."

Sarah glared at her. "You can fall apart later. Right now, I need you." She nodded towards his head. She started compressions and stopped at fifteen. "Now."

Parker fell to her knees, tilting his head back. She pinched his nose with one hand, and using her other hand, she opened his mouth and breathed two breaths into his mouth. When she was finished, Sarah started the compressions again, followed by more breaths.

Three minutes later, Sarah's arms shook with exhaustion. She prayed for strength, not excepting defeat.

She watched Parker out of the corner of her eyes. Silent tears streamed down Parker's face and Sarah understood that her calling was not Parker's, and it had been her own selfishness that blinded her to Parker's suffering. She knew this had been incredibly hard on Parker, and she wished she could say something to make it better. Instead, she buried her thoughts in the task at hand.

Two more minutes and nothing, no movement, no breathing, only stillness. Sarah cried out in frustration. "Come on! Fight, God damn it!" Her frustration compounded by her newfound guilt made her shake violently. "You can't fucking die on us!" She felt fear coursing through her veins, igniting a growing rage. Eight years hadn't helped it get any better. No, people were still dying all around her.

She reared up and in a furious state, slammed her fist down on his chest. She nearly fell over in shock when his body lurched up and he started coughing. Nervous laughter filled her ears and she realized it was her own. She leaned over him, waiting for the coughing to stop. "Sir? Sir? Just lie still. Parker, go grab my jacket out of the car."

When she brought the coat back, Sarah folded it up and laid it under his head.

He had started to sit up and Sarah gently pushed against his shoulders. "Just lie still."

"What…what happened?"

"There was a tornado. It leveled your house. We managed to dig you out."

"My…my house?" His eyes looked confused. "Trailer. I live in a trailer."

Sarah's eyes scanned the debris. Even with unidentifiable piles of wood, concrete and metal, she could tell there were no trailers near here.

"Sir, where exactly is your house?"

His brow furrowed and his eyes searched hers for answers. Finding none, he willed his brain to function again.

Realization dawned in his eyes. "The last thing I remember is the tornado ripping the roof off my trailer and I couldn't hold on any longer."

Sarah realized that against all odds, the tornado had actually pulled him from the trailer and carried him here. "Where is your trailer? Give me a landmark."

"Water tower. It's next to the water tower."

She scanned the skyline for a water tower and her eyes widened when she saw what was left of it. The top had been ripped away. What had shocked her the most was that she judged it to be at least a half a mile away from her present spot.

"Holy shit!" Parker said in awe. "That means he was in the tornado?"

"I think so." Sarah shook her head. This was first for her, another in a long line of them today. How he survived was beyond her. He almost hadn't, if not for her and Parker. The feeling that this man's life had been in their hands humbled her more than she'd ever been.

He had started coughing again, probably from dust that had blown into his throat during his ride in the tornado.

Sarah helped him up and studied his face. He still looked stunned, but alert, which was a good sign. She wanted to interview him, the business part of her acknowledging that this would guarantee her at least one more year of funding, and she needed the backing to continue. Besides, a piece like this on *Rogue Weather* would be huge.

She asked Parker to get the camera and while she was away, asked him if he would let her interview him. He merely shook his head and she said a silent thank you, knowing that had he been fully alert, he would have realized that telling his story of riding a tornado would have garnered him a pretty big paycheck. Her guilt got the better of her, and she acknowledged the fact that she would see to it that he was paid handsomely for this piece.

Hours later, when they watched the playback and she allowed herself to see the destruction, she realized that once again, all that she'd pursued up till now, could never have prepared her for what they had witnessed today. It also made her even more determined to find a way to make sure that no town suffered like this one did.

Chapter 18

Remy cleared her throat loudly. Parker had the decency to at least look chagrined. "Couple hours, okay?"

"Yeah." Parker held up her hand. "I don't suppose getting your own room is an option."

"Not on my budget." Remy said with a smile. "But, since you asked so nicely, I'll give you three hours instead of two."

Parker winked and grabbed Carmen around the waist. She furrowed her brows at Remy. "How about now?"

Remy shook her head and laughed. "I can take a hint." She grabbed a sweatshirt and pulled the door closed behind her. The storms had left a distinct chill in the air, and she donned the sweatshirt before she went any further.

"Hey."

Remy turned and smiled when she saw Sarah walking towards her. "Hey, yourself."

"Where you headed?"

"I'm not sure." Remy shrugged. "Hadn't exactly made up my mind."

"Want some company?" Sarah hoped the answer was yes, and yet, something in Remy's eyes made her feel some trepidation. "I'm sorry. Maybe you want to be alone."

Remy stopped and put her hand on Sarah's arm. "Not really. I'd rather have company…especially yours."

Sarah let out a breath, relief on her face. "Me too. I mean, I'd rather have company."

Remy quirked an eyebrow. "Just not mine?"

"That's not what I said." Sarah's eyes flashed defensively. "Don't put words in my mouth."

"Look, I'm sorry." Remy smiled ruefully. "It's been a really stressful day, and I'm just a little on edge."

Sarah put her hand up dismissively. "Don't apologize. I know what you mean."

"So, you want to grab a bite to eat?" Remy smirked. "I'll show you mine, if you show me yours."

Sarah rolled her eyes. "You never give up do you?"

"What?" Remy feigned innocence. "I meant I'd tell you my adventure today, if you tell me yours."

"Mmm—hmmm." Sarah looked askance at her. "Feed me first then we'll see about sharing."

"Fair enough." Remy steered them towards Sarah's car. "Mind if we take yours? I don't feel like driving the beast tonight."

"Sure. But, will you drive?" Sarah tossed the keys towards Remy, and she caught them with ease. She waited while Remy unlocked the car and held the door open for her. "Thanks."

"Sure." Remy ran around the other side, and after adjusting the seat to accommodate her longer legs, eased out of the parking lot and into traffic. They'd gone east of the tornadoes to find a spot for the night. They had made it almost to Atlanta before they found an area that had power and empty rooms. It had been years since Remy had been there, and it took her a few moments to find her bearings.

"What are you feeling?" Sarah watched the scenery fly by. She was no stranger to this town. Nashville was close enough that she and her college roommates had frequented some of the seedier bars in their heyday.

"Honestly? I really want a burger."

Sarah clapped her hands together. "That sounds fabulous and I know the perfect place."

"Then point me in the right direction 'cause I am starving."

Fifteen minutes later, Remy parked the car in front of Grindhouse Killer Burgers. "Looks promising."

Sarah grabbed her hand and pulled her along excitedly. "Arguably the best burger joint in Atlanta."

"Do I dare ask how you know about this place?" Remy shot Sarah a sideways glance as she held open the door for her.

"Nothing exciting. My college girlfriends and I used to drive down here to party."

"Oh, come down here for a rave or two?"

Sarah started laughing out loud. "Umm, not exactly. I wouldn't call myself the techno party animal."

"Hmmm." Remy didn't say anything more than that. She'd been to a rave or two years ago and something told her Sarah wasn't that type.

They were seated after a short wait and Remy eyed the menu. "Peanut butter on a burger? I'm starting to doubt your restaurant picking skills."

"Shut up." Sarah slapped her arm. "It's actually really good."

Remy quirked an eyebrow skeptically. "I'll take your word for it."

"Fair enough. I'm getting it though and you are going to taste mine."

Remy waggled her eyebrows lasciviously.

"No, no, no. That's not what I meant." Sarah could feel her cheeks warm briefly, and she worked to keep the blush in check. "Don't you ever get tired of this cat and mouse game?"

"No." Remy shook her head. "I would only tire of it if I thought there was a chance I wouldn't catch you."

Sarah rolled her eyes. "Pretty sure of yourself, aren't you?"

"No." Remy's eyes were suddenly serious. "I have to believe that fate brought us together for a reason. I just have to wait patiently for you to realize it."

"Oh." Sarah couldn't hide the shock at her honesty. She was realizing that with each passing day, Remy was making it very hard for her to keep her promise to herself. She was saved from further feelings of self—doubt by their waitress.

She set beers in front of both of them and smiled. "Y'all ready to order?"

Remy nodded. "I think so. You want to go first?"

"I'll take the Peanut Butter Burger."

"Good choice." The waitress turned her attention to Remy, and in a move that was obvious to both of them, gave her an appraising once over. "For you, darlin'?"

Remy smiled flirtatiously. Maybe this was just what she needed to push Sarah over the edge. A little green—eyed jealousy. "I'll have the Jose Mendoza. Extra bacon."

"Sure thing, honey." The waitress licked her lips and sauntered off with a wink.

"Really?" Sarah rolled her eyes and groaned loudly. "Should I take a cab home?"

"No." Remy said with a laugh. "Not interested, anyway."

"Could have fooled me."

"Jealous?" Remy said with an unspoken challenge. "You don't need to be. My heart belongs to you."

"No, of course not." Sarah's voice raised an octave, and she hoped that Remy couldn't tell she was lying. "Why would I be jealous?"

Remy shrugged. "No reason. Guess I read it wrong."

"So, tell me about your day." Sarah suggested, trying to steer the conversation away from them and into safer territory.

Remy shook her head slowly. She wrung her hands together. Today had been hard, harder than she had experienced in a long time. Emotionally, she was spent. "Rough to say the least. I didn't think I would live to see a day like today. I've never seen that many tornadoes, and never that many EF5's."

"Tell me about it." Sarah agreed readily. "The cities...the cities were wiped out. Birmingham was a war zone."

"Tuscaloosa too."

"I'm going to remember this day for a long time. I wish you could have seen the guy that got lifted up in the tornado. Craziest thing I've ever seen."

"Are you serious?" Remy's eyes flashed in disbelief.

"Totally. Might be a few days before he remembers exactly what happened."

"I'll be damned." Remy shook her head, trying to picture it. "Carmen and I pulled a little girl out from under a mattress that a tree had fallen on. Amazingly enough, she was okay. I'm just sad to say, not everyone was that lucky. No matter how hard we try and how much data we get, we just can't seem to get a head of the storms."

"No, but you're trying." Sarah's hand covered Remy's. "I know it breaks your heart every time someone dies. You take it personally, like you've lost them. It's not your fault, Rem. Some things you can't control."

"I know. I tell myself that, but it doesn't make it any less personal to me." Remy rubbed the back of her neck, the tension making her head hurt slightly. "Every single one cuts right into me, just like the first time."

"I know, but you can't blame yourself. At least, you're doing something about it. Not burying your head in the sand and hoping someone else comes up with a way to save people." Sarah squeezed her hand and tried to ignore the jolt that shot up her arm and into her heart. She pulled her hand away quickly then frowned at the obviousness of her gesture.

She had to get herself under control. She refused to let herself fall for Remy. She kept repeating that mantra to herself and hoped it wasn't too late. "What we do isn't easy, and I have a lot of respect for you. You are an amazing woman, Remy. I'm here today because of you and your heartfelt desire to help people. That says a lot."

"Thanks." Remy shrugged. "You know seeing what happened today made me really think about how short life can be. You never know what tomorrow will bring, if you're lucky enough to get a tomorrow. I have to learn to live each day to the fullest. Carmen teases me all the time. She says I'm so focused on what we do that I forget who I am and I forget to live."

"She's right." Sarah teased. "Your focus is so intense. Like a laser beam focused on a tiny point in the distance. It's almost scary."

"Scary, how?" Remy's eyes showed her confusion.

"Mmm, it's hard to explain. It's almost like you're focused and intense like a black hole, and if I don't be careful, I'll get pulled in." Sarah shuddered at the sudden realization. That's how she felt. Pulled towards a force so strong that she couldn't resist even if she wanted to. Yet, the fear she knew she should have felt didn't come. Instead, she almost felt serene. She imagined it was the calm a swimmer felt when they stopped fighting against the undertow and let the ocean send them where they could swim to safety. That's what she would do. Just stop fighting and wait till she floated to safety.

"Sounds insanely unromantic." Remy smiled ruefully. "No wonder C gives me such a hard time." She paused as the waitress set plates in front of them, piled high with burgers and what seemed to be a bottomless pile of fries.

"Can I get you ladies anything else?" She directed the comment at them both, but her gaze rested on Remy.

"No thanks. I think we're good."

She smiled. "If you need anything, darlin', just holler. I'm at your beck and call." She winked again and walked away.

"*I'm at your beck and call.*" Sarah said mockingly. "I'll just bet she is."

Remy smiled. "I already told you I'm not interested."

"What gives with you anyway? What happened to the consummate player?" Sarah shot her a querulous look. "Where's the girl that talked me into bed in less than two hours?"

"Oh, you want that woman?" Remy waggled a fry towards Sarah. "That can be very easily arranged."

"No, that's not what I meant, and you know it." Sarah pinched the bridge of her nose. Damn Remy for being irresistibly cute. "I just meant here's all this talk about opening your eyes and seeing the world around you, and instead, you seem to be withdrawing."

"Just because I'm not whoring around anymore doesn't mean I don't notice what's around me. I notice you."

Sarah shook her head. "And, there she is."

Remy chuckled softly. "I can't help it if the first thing I notice when I open my eyes is you."

"You're incorrigible."

"True, but you love me anyway." Remy said it with such childlike innocence that anyone listening would have thought she was just teasing. Sarah saw the heat that flashed in her eyes, and she shuddered all the way down to her toes.

Sarah took a long drink of her beer, willing the liquid to cool the heat that was building deep inside her. "So, you want to taste my burger?" She waived the Peanut Butter Burger in Remy's face, teasing her to try it.

"Yes. I want to taste it." Remy's voice was husky, and Sarah knew, without a doubt, the *it* she was talking about was not her burger. She gulped nervously as Remy took the burger from her hand and instead of taking a bite, put her mouth around Sarah's finger and swirled her tongue around it.

Sarah nearly fainted from the intimate gesture, and before she swooned, had the good nature to pull away from those tantalizing lips and that dangerous tongue. "What was that for?"

"Peanut butter…on your finger." Remy said innocently, as if that explained what had just transpired between them. "And, you're right. It does taste very good." She could see Sarah's hand shaking on the table. She was happy to see that it had affected Sarah as much as it had her. It took all she had to keep from reaching across the table and kissing Sarah right there.

"I…I…" Sarah's next words were a jumbled mess. The shock of what had happened gave way to the heat of the moment, and right now, it was making her blood boil. She finally got herself together enough to frown her mock disapproval at Remy. "So, that's a no to the burger?"

Remy shook her head from side—to—side. "It would pale in comparison to my first taste."

Sarah put her face down, not wanting Remy to see her blush again. She needed to get a grip. A few words, and Remy making love to her finger had her ready for another roll in the sack. She ate the rest of her burger quietly, pretending to study the restaurant. Several minutes later, she wiped her mouth and threw her napkin on the table. "That was ridiculously good."

Remy took that as her cue that the conversation would not return to them. "Great choice."

As they walked back to the car, she had to shove her hands in her pockets to keep from grabbing Sarah's hand. When Sarah had covered hers at the table, Remy's blood pressure had spiked wildly, and when she'd licked the peanut butter off Sarah's finger, she had nearly lost it. This cat and mouse game, as Sarah called it, was really getting to her. She had only to look at Sarah, and her mind immediately flashed to that night. She could still feel the warmth of their naked bodies melded together. Perfectly, she might add. "Anywhere else?"

Sarah shook her head. "No, I'm kind of tired." She needed to get some space between them. She couldn't stop looking at Remy's lips and thinking about kissing her. The kiss the other night had opened up a floodgate of emotions. She felt them tingle and knew she had to get away fast, or she was going to do something stupid. "Just back to the hotel."

Remy merely nodded. Her heart jumped. Nothing had happened, but she felt different. Felt the air between them sizzle with unspoken heat. She knew Sarah's heart had made its choice. Now, she had to be patient and wait while her head caught up.

Chapter 19

Remy handed Sarah her keys and waited for her to open the door to her hotel room. "Thanks for dinner."

"You're welcome." Unconsciously, Sarah moved closer to Remy, feeling the heat emanating from her body. "I'm sorry you have to waste your time on me."

Remy shook her head from side—to—side. "If all I had was time, I'd waste it on you."

Sarah's heart thudded in her chest. Without trying, Remy was pulling her in, making her feel things she had promised herself she wouldn't feel. "Remy, please forget about me. Forget about us."

"I can't. I've tried for the last eight years to get you out of my head. Can't do it."

Sarah rubbed her palm on Remy's cheek. "I haven't forgotten you either, but I can't let you in. So, please, forget about us."

Remy leaned into Sarah's palm. "I'm sorry."

"For what?"

"This." Remy turned her head sideways and kissed Sarah's palm. She put her hand over Sarah's and held her there against her lips. She kissed her wrist and felt Sarah shudder against her.

Remy's lips were soft and warm and Sarah's skin tingled at the contact. "Remy, what are you doing?" Sarah's strangled voice was low and raspy.

"I'm forgetting." Remy squeezed Sarah's hand and pulled Sarah's body flush against hers. She cupped Sarah's face in her palms and pressed her lips against Sarah's softly. She heard a moan and her mind couldn't tell if it was her or Sarah. She teased Sarah's lips with her tongue, seeking entry. When her lips finally parted, Remy slid her tongue over her bottom lip seductively. Her lips were soft and inviting. She knew she could get lost kissing Sarah.

Sarah felt the world swirling around her, her knees unsteady. She put her arms around Remy and held her tightly. Remy's lips pressed against hers. Their tongues tangling together was making the blood pound in her ears. Her stomach fluttered pleasantly and she shivered, remembering their first time together. She returned Remy's kiss with abandon, not sure she could resist even if she tried. When her senses finally came back to her, she put her hands on Remy's shoulders and pushed her away, but didn't break their embrace.

Remy searched her face, looking for regret but found none. "I'm sorry, Sarah. I can't just walk away. Something keeps bringing us back together, and I don't want to fight it anymore."

"I'm scared." Sarah's eyes welled up. She wiped away a tear before it had a chance to escape.

"Don't be." Remy wrapped her arms around Sarah. "I promise I won't hurt you."

Sarah shook her head from side—to—side. "No one can make that promise."

"I can." Remy swallowed. "At least, I can promise not to hurt you intentionally."

Emotions swirled around in Sarah's head, her heart in a vise grip. "Why couldn't you just make this easier on us and run the other way?"

"Because, I love you."

Remy felt a huge wave of relief sweep over her. The truth was out. She had felt the feeling for a long time now, she just hadn't known what name to give it and now she did. She loved Sarah, loved her with her whole being. Her heart was in Sarah's hands now and she prayed that it wouldn't be returned a broken, shattered mess.

Remy's naked admission was more than Sarah could bear. She pressed her body to Remy's, her arms holding her tight. Her blood was churning in her veins and she held her breath, willing her heart to slow down. It didn't matter though, she couldn't stop the influx of desire that made her body vibrate. She could pretend, keep denying the feelings, but she could no longer keep her body in check. She wanted Remy with everything she had, and tonight, she would give herself physically, even if she couldn't let her heart go. "You know, I can't love you. At least, not yet."

"Yes." Remy whispered against her ear softly. "But, I can wait. I've waited eight years, what's a couple more?" She kissed her temple and caressed it with her cheek. "Please say you won't make me wait that long to touch you again."

Sarah tried to quell the butterflies in her stomach. Desire shot through her veins and her clit tingled. She couldn't remember the last time that someone had made her body react so quickly. It was never like that with anyone…except Remy. All these years between them, and while her mind hadn't remembered every touch, her body had. As much as she wasn't ready to admit it, her heart hadn't forgotten either.

Sarah glanced at Remy and the look of raw desire pierced her to the core. No, tonight she would no longer deny what had been building between them for years. She didn't say a word. There were none that could capture what she felt right now. She took Remy's hand and put it on her breast.

The fullness of Sarah's breast in her hand made her body quiver uncontrollably. She remembered Sarah's taste and her mouth watered. She swallowed and let out a breath. Eight years of waiting had brought them to this magical place, and suddenly, Remy was afraid too. What if she gave her heart and Sarah didn't love her back? She felt Sarah move against her and suddenly it didn't matter. All that mattered was the woman in her arms and making her happy.

She caressed Sarah's breast and felt her nipple harden against her palm. She watched in awe as Sarah's brown eyes darkened to black pools of desire. Remy felt a need so primal surge through her body, and she sought Sarah's mouth with hers. She plunged her tongue into Sarah's mouth, and their tongues danced together hungrily. She felt shocks of pleasure shoot to her extremities.

Remy pulled Sarah's shirt from her jeans and caressed her skin lightly. "You're just as soft as I remember you."

Sarah moaned loudly when Remy undid her bra and cupped her breasts. She felt Remy's thumbs rub circles around her nipples, and they were immediately hard. It was like this with her the first time too. One touch and Remy could bring her to her knees. "God, you were the only one that could make me almost come just from a touch."

Remy chuckled. "I've never wanted to give a woman pleasure like I do you. Your breasts are perfect. So full, so soft." She pulled Sarah's shirt over her head and tossed it on the chair. Her bra was discarded just as quickly. "Mmmm, so perfect." She pulled Sarah's nipple into her mouth and flicked her tongue across it. She was rewarded with a deep growl from Sarah.

Sarah pulled away and tugged at Remy's shirt. "Take this off. I want to feel your body against mine."

Remy pulled her sweatshirt off and Sarah's breath caught in her throat. Remy was not wearing a bra and her small breasts begged to be touched. Sarah caught Remy's breast in her hand and teased her nipple until it was taut against her palm. "Looks like you haven't forgotten."

"I told you, I could never forget you...no matter how hard I tried." She pulled Sarah's hand against her heart and held it there. "Let's just say a long time ago you got in here, and I haven't been able to shake you."

Sarah smiled sweetly. "I didn't mean too."

"It's okay. You did it without even trying."

Sarah's breath caught again. Remy continued to amaze her. She could melt her heart with just a word. She knew she didn't stand a chance of not falling in love with her. She pulled Remy into her arms, and when their breasts brushed together, she felt her clit tighten again. She was aching for Remy's touch.

Remy read the emotion on Sarah's face, and she pulled her towards the bed. Her eyes were dark pools of desire, but there was something more hidden behind her need. Remy wouldn't give a name to it, but she felt some of her fears fading away. Sarah may not realize it yet, but she was falling for her, and Remy was content to wait.

"Can I?" Sarah nodded and Remy undid the button on Sarah's jeans and eased them over her hips. She saw a wet spot on her panties, and her knees almost buckled. She wrapped her arms around Sarah's waist and steadied herself. She could feel strength coming from Sarah's body. She kissed her stomach softly and chuckled when Sarah tried to pull away. "Still ticklish, I see?"

Sarah shot her a look. "Still trying to torture me, I see?"

"Maybe." Remy smirked. "But, I seem to remember foreplay was quite fun with you."

"If by foreplay, you mean hours of making love to me with your eyes, then yes, foreplay was quite fun." She shoved Remy's hand into her panties. "Eight years of foreplay is enough for tonight. I want you inside me."

Remy's fingers found her center and stroked her wetness. She sucked in a breath. Sarah's body welcomed her, and she felt reason taking second place to her primal needs. "Fuck, Sarah. You're so wet. So wet for me."

"Mmmm." Sarah moaned softly. "It seems I've been that way for some time now. Damn you for being so incredibly sexy." She ran her hands through Remy's hair and pulled her mouth down on hers. The time for going slow was gone now. Her body was no longer her own, and Remy's hands on her and inside her sent sparks shooting through her veins. "I need you to make me come."

Remy merely nodded. She pulled the covers back and laid Sarah down on the mattress. Her eyes roamed over Sarah's body hungrily. She was soft in all the right places, her body so gently curved it made Remy ache to touch her. She didn't realize she'd licked her lips until Sarah nudged her with her knee and smiled. "I taste much better than I look."

Remy gulped and smiled ruefully. "Sorry, I'm etching this moment into my memory."

"Baby, if you hurry up and get in this bed, I'll give you something way better to remember."

Remy didn't remember Sarah being so vocal, but they had both grown up and had other lovers. She didn't imagine that Sarah hadn't picked up a few things along the way. She pulled her panties over her hips, inhaling her scent. Remy growled under her breath. She wanted to taste her now, but she pulled back, willing herself to be patient.

Sarah watched Remy undress, unable to breath. The long muscles in her body rippled beneath her skin. Her body still looked like a swimmer. Long and lean and dangerously sexy. Remy knelt over her, and Sarah pushed at her chest, stopping her. She eyed her black briefs and shook her head. "Uh—uh, I want those off too. I want to feel how wet I make you."

Remy's arms shook violently. She was dripping wet already and she had only touched Sarah. If wet was what Sarah wanted then wet she would get. Finally naked, she knelt on the bed. She was poised over Sarah's glistening center, and once again, she forced herself not to take her in her mouth. She eased her body over Sarah's, and she let out a low moan.

"Mmm, you feel so good against me." Sarah cupped Remy's bottom and pulled her closer, feeling wetness against her body. She stuck her hand between their bodies and slid her fingers along Remy's slick folds. She could feel Remy's clit hard against her fingers, and the corners of her mouth turned up. "God, you're wet." She swirled her fingers around Remy's clit once more then pulled her fingers out and rubbed them over Remy's lips. She kissed Remy and nipped her bottom lip. She smiled lasciviously. "And, you taste so good."

Remy shuddered again, the length of her body covering Sarah's. She started to move against her, feeling their moist centers brushing together. She covered Sarah's mouth with hers, her lips still moist from her own juices. She tasted sweet and salty, and the thought of tasting herself made her stomach jump wildly. She ran her tongue over Sarah's jawline and swirled it around her ear. When she spoke, her voice was husky. "Now, it's my turn, darlin'."

Sarah turned her head and felt Remy drop kisses down her neck and across her chest. She caught her nipple between her teeth and nipped it gently. Sarah nearly came off the bed.

"Too much?" Remy asked softly.

"No." Sarah arched towards her. "But, if you keep that up, I won't be able to last much longer."

Remy planted a kiss on her other breast. "Then I guess I should stop. I want you to come in my mouth." She slid down Sarah's body, her hands teasing her breasts as her lips trailed kisses over her stomach and hips. She felt Sarah's legs widen, and she settled between them, her mouth immediately watering at the scent of Sarah's arousal. She could see how wet Sarah was, and it made her own clit harden to an achingly hard knob.

Sarah arched her hips towards Remy. "Please, I need you inside me now."

Remy licked the vee between her legs and blew on her clit, watching it pulse wildly. She ran her tongue along the wet folds, tasting Sarah's sweet nectar. Too long, she had been denied this feast, and now, she would take her fill. She plunged her tongue into Sarah's warm center and felt Sarah's body contract around her. She plunged her tongue as deep as she could, taking as much of Sarah's sweet juices as she could.

Sarah's breath was ragged. Remy's tongue inside her was making her blood pound. She could feel it pulsating in her clit, her orgasm building deep within. It had been exactly eight years since her body had felt such blinding pleasure. Her need was insatiable. She felt like she would come out of her skin at any minute, the overwhelming need to explode driving her higher and higher. "Please, Remy, I need to come."

Remy's mouth stilled for a brief second. Her mind reeled. She was making love to the woman she had dreamed of for the last eight years. Their one night together had set them on a parallel journey, and finally, it had come full circle. She felt Sarah arch against her mouth and reeled her mind back in. She ran her fingers over Sarah's slick folds and felt her own orgasm dangerously close. She caught Sarah's clit in her mouth and sucked gently, swirling her tongue around it, feeling it grow inside her. She slid one finger inside Sarah's body and held it there, waiting for her to relax and open up to her.

Sarah felt her muscles contract around Remy, and she took several deep breaths, wanting more of her inside. "More."

Remy heard the single word and her stomach jumped. She pulled her finger out and slid two in. She withdrew them only to plunge them in again, feeling Sarah's hips raise to meet her movements. She quickened her movements, and soon, she could feel Sarah's body beginning to tighten against her.

Sarah's body thrummed with pleasure. She could feel the ache begin low in her belly and work its way through her veins. She knew she was going to come soon. She tensed, her body hanging on, waiting for the moment when her pleasure would send her over the edge. "Harder, Remy." She arched her hips, driving Remy deeper and deeper into her body. She felt the first waves of pleasure begin in her clit and she held her breath.

Remy brushed against a spot deep within Sarah's aroused center and stroked even more pleasure from her shaking body. She felt her tense and shudder twice against her, her mouth never leaving Sarah's clit. She rode every ebb and flow of Sarah's orgasm, driving her body to the edge and sent her hurtling over, her screams music to Remy's ears.

When Sarah finally caught her breath, she moaned deeply. "What did you do to me?"

"Only what I've wanted to do ever since the morning you kicked me out."

Remy's smile was so heartfelt and innocent that Sarah couldn't help but melt a little more. She grabbed her hand and tugged her back up over her body. "Then it's only fair you let me do what I've been thinking about doing since the day I met you." She slid her fingers into Remy's body and caught Remy's lip between hers, sucking gently.

Remy moved against Sarah's fingers, her own orgasm so close she knew it wouldn't take much. She pushed her body up and slid down Sarah's fingers, driving them deep inside her body. She started a slow, rhythmic dance and when Sarah brushed her thumb over her clit, she cried out, unable to stop the pleasure that rippled through her body.

Chapter 20

Remy kissed Sarah's nose and sat back against the headboard, waiting for her to wake up. She smiled when her brown eyes opened, drowsy and definitely sated looking. "Good morning, Bonneville."

Sarah sat up and took the coffee cup, inhaling its rich scent. She took a sip and smiled thankfully. "You brought me coffee, I won't kill you for calling me that."

"Well, if you did, I would die a happy woman." Remy teased and brushed her knuckles against Sarah's jaw.

Sarah blushed. She flashed back to last night, and a brief glance at the clock, told her she'd only been asleep for a couple of hours. She couldn't help it, one taste of Remy and she had been insatiable, only stopping when Remy told her she would die if she came again. "About last night."

Remy quirked an eyebrow and waited for her world to drop out from under her. "Yes?" She cleared her throat, her voice trembling.

Sarah saw the fear in her eyes and her heart broke for Remy. Remy was unsure because of her. She found Remy's hand and squeezed it reassuringly. "I was just going to say last night was amazing, but…"

Remy sucked in, not realizing she had been holding her breath. She wasn't normally this anxious, but she was learning quickly that Sarah had a way of keeping her on edge. She saw Sarah's smile and relaxed a bit. "But?"

"But…don't expect every night to be like last night. I need sleep." Sarah's tone was stern, but her eyes danced mischievously.

"So, marathon sessions of making love are out? Check." Remy made a tick mark in the air.

"Well, not out, per se." Sarah sat up and crossed her legs under her. "Just not every night."

"Oh yeah? I seem to remember someone couldn't take no for an answer last night." Remy waggled her eyebrows at Sarah and was rewarded with a punch in the arm. "It's true. I remember trying to cut you off after the fifth time last night."

Sarah set her coffee on the nightstand and pushed herself up on her knees. Her breasts brushed against Remy's face provocatively. She rubbed her nipple over Remy's lips, pulling away when Remy tried to capture it in her mouth. "Are you thinking of saying no now?"

Remy groaned loudly and wrapped her arms around Sarah, pulling her body against hers. She mumbled something unintelligible into her breasts. She flicked her tongue over Sarah's nipple, feeling her shudder in her arms. "No is the furthest thing from my mind right now."

A loud knock on the door made them both jump. "Damn it. Saved by the bell, but you're in a lot of trouble later."

Remy kissed her on the lips. "I'll hold you to that." She watched Sarah grab her clothes and run into the bathroom before she opened the door. She blushed at the smirk on Parker's face.

"Good morning." Parker teased. She followed Remy into the room and paused by the bed, her eyes taking in the mess. "Guess you found overnight accommodations."

"Uh, yeah. Sarah was nice enough to let me sleep here. Thought you two could use a night alone."

"Well, wasn't that sweet of her?" Parker ran her hand over the comforter with another smirk. "Looks like you were nice and cozy."

Remy felt the heat rise in her face. She pulled at her collar, suddenly hot. She cleared her throat loudly. "Yep, nice and cozy. Slept like a baby."

"Uh—huh." Parker saw the panties lying on the floor, discarded haphazardly in last night's haste. She crossed her arms over her chest and pierced Remy with a sharp gaze, her eyes dancing mischievously.

Remy glanced at Sarah's panties and swallowed nervously. She knew that Parker knew what had happened, and there was no point in trying to deny it. One look at Parker, and Remy knew she was enjoying making her uncomfortable. "Umm, I should probably get going. Sarah, Parker is here."

Sarah left her at Parker's mercy for several more minutes before she came out to rescue her. "Hey, Parker."

A look passed between them and had it been anyone besides Remy, they may have passed it off as an innocent look between cousins. But, Remy saw the meaning buried underneath the exchange, and she knew without words that Parker had given her silent approval. She shot Sarah an apologetic smile, sorry that they had been interrupted. "I should go. Thanks for last night."

Sarah saw the emotions in Remy's eyes, and she wished they were alone so she could give her a proper goodbye. They ran into each other frequently, but there was no guarantee they would always end up in the same place. It could be weeks before she saw her again, much less had the chance to kiss her. She shot Parker a look.

Parker got her meaning. "I'm gonna grab some coffee." She nodded towards the cups on the nightstand. "You want anything?"

"A Dew please." Sarah looked up at Remy. "You want more coffee since yours is cold now?"

"Nah, I'm good. Thanks, though."

Parker walked out and left the two women alone.

Remy cleared her throat. "Seriously, thank you for last night."

Without a word, Sarah slipped into her arms and snuggled her cheek against Remy's shoulder. "You're welcome. I, I forgot how good you feel."

Remy's heart thudded against her chest. It wasn't a confession of love, but she would take it. She knew Sarah was still struggling with her feelings for her, and she wasn't ready to accept that she was in love with Remy. "Don't forget."

Sarah pulled back and smiled up at Remy. "I won't, not this time." She kissed Remy quickly and stepped away. "Goodbye, Remy."

Remy leaned against the doorframe and sent Sarah a smile that made Sarah's knees buckle. In that moment, Sarah thought her devastatingly handsome, and she knew her heart was no longer hers.

"See ya next trip, Bonneville."

When Parker came back, she found Sarah towel drying her hair. She set her Mt. Dew on the bathroom counter and leaned against the door watching her cousin. She almost chuckled at the faraway look in Sarah's eyes, but she stopped herself in time. "Sleep well?"

"What?" Sarah regarded Parker quizzically, as if just realizing she wasn't alone in the room. "Oh yeah, slept great."

Parker shoved off the door and rubbed a spot on Sarah's chin.

Sarah quirked an eyebrow. "What was that for?"

"Wiping off the drool." Parker smirked, her eyes dancing. "You're going to have to wipe the smile off your face, if you want us to believe nothing happened."

"Nothing did…" Sarah stopped and she caught her reflection in the mirror. She may be able to tell a lie, but her eyes couldn't. They were silently televising all her innermost thoughts. "Okay, fine. We slept together. Are you happy?"

"Depends." Parker shrugged. "Are you happy?"

Sarah's smile grew wider. "Yeah, I am. She makes me happy."

"Bueno. You deserve to be happy, Chica."

"My, my, bilingual now, eh?"

"My, my, Canadian now, eh?" Parker teased. "I guess I have a little Spanish in me."

Sarah rolled her eyes. "Really?"

Parker smirked. "Hey, you might be into total non—disclosure, but I'm proud of my Puerto Rican and her umm, Latin sex drive. I can't help it if she makes me want to brag a little."

"Or, a lot." Sarah ran a brush through her hair and pulled it into a small ponytail. "So, you're in love, huh?"

Parker blushed and shook her head. She couldn't keep the smile from creeping across her face. "Very much so. She's the one."

"So you've said." Sarah squeezed past Parker and stopped in front of her small suitcase. "Kind of quick, don't you think?"

Parker shrugged. "What's time when it's right? I knew the second I met Carmen." She could feel the heat in her cheeks and she didn't care. "She's different, Sarah. Not like the women back home. You know how it is."

Sarah nodded. She was well aware of the lesbian scene in her hometown. She liked to tease that she lived in a very green town. Most of the lesbians liked to recycle their women, which meant that everyone in the small town they lived in had slept with everyone else. It reminded her of the old game *Six Degrees of Kevin Bacon,* only she could link them all in two to three steps. "I forget about that being on the road all the time. Evan should have been a good reminder of that though."

"True. She's a bitch." Parker's tone was venomous.

"Wow, tell me how you really feel." Sarah pulled a clean tee shirt on.

Parker smiled ruefully. "Well, she is." She watched Sarah's face for her reaction. When she saw none, she smiled. Obviously, she was good and over Evan. "Remy's good people, you know."

Sarah looked up surprise on her face. "I'm starting to realize that."

Parker narrowed her eyes. "She loves you, you know? You should be careful not to mess this up."

"What do you mean?" Sarah's brow wrinkled in confusion. "Mess this up how?"

"I know you, Cuz. You don't let people in. You barely let me in and that's only because I bugged the crap out of you till you caved. Don't put up the famous Sarah wall and push her away."

"I do not do that!" Sarah stopped suddenly. Was Parker right? Did she keep herself locked up and not let anyone in? She thought back to her previous relationships, romantic or otherwise, and she couldn't pick one that was more than skin deep. "Oh."

"Oh is right." Parker smiled apologetically. "Don't end up an old lady, lonely and alone, because you can't let her in."

Sarah opened her mouth to object then shut it quickly. She didn't want to admit it, but Parker was right. She didn't let people in. She had kept Remy at arms' length. Remy said she was in love with her, and she couldn't reciprocate it. She made love with her all night long, and she had kept a part of herself locked away. She hadn't given Remy all of herself, and she was suddenly left wondering if she could do that. Could she open up and let her in completely?

Sarah shook her head. She wasn't sure. She knew she needed to, or Parker's words would be more than idle chatter. They would be a foreboding harbinger of her life to come. She realized, for the first time, that growing up in a household that never shared their feelings had left her facing life with a gigantic cocoon around her and wondering if she had the strength to break free from it and let someone love her completely.

Chapter 21

Carmen flipped the computer off and got out to stretch her legs. "Can you believe this shit? Two weeks and nothing. It's like the storms decided to go on vacation."

Remy shrugged. "It's nothing new. We've seen that before."

"Not that long, Chica."

"2006." Remy offered nonchalantly. They went five weeks without seeing a tornado at all. She knew what was eating at Carmen. It had been three weeks since they had met up with Sarah and Parker. Phone sex just wasn't cutting it for Carmen anymore. Remy hadn't even had the luxury of that, which given how wound up she was right now, she would have settled for that.

What she had gotten plenty of was long phone conversations with Sarah. Just thinking of her voice on the other end of the line made her stomach tighten. There wasn't much they didn't know about each other at this point. That thought made Remy smile.

Remy glanced up at Carmen, who was tapping her foot impatiently against the curb, watching Remy pump gas. "You know you don't have to stand there bitching about it, you could make yourself useful."

Carmen quirked an eyebrow threateningly, and Remy had to cover a smirk. Much as Carmen wanted to be a badass, she was the furthest thing from that. Certainly, she could shout with the best of them, and even that wasn't scary since Remy didn't understand half of what she was saying anyway.

"You can finish filling up Thor or grab me a coke...pretty please." Remy saw her eyes narrow and decided softening her up a little might help.

"Oh, fine." Carmen said with a huff. She pushed off the truck and headed into the gas station, a string of Spanish profanities trailing over her shoulder.

Remy could only shake her head and laugh. She watched the meter inch its way towards one hundred dollars, silently cursing the cost of diesel these days. She was just tightening the gas gap when her pocket started vibrating. Dusting off her hands, she pulled her phone out and hit the accept button, a huge grin on her face. "Hey."

"Straw."

"Huh?" Remy wrinkled her brow.

"Sorry." Sarah said with a chuckle. *"I thought we were playing the word game. You know, say something, and I say the first thing that comes to my mind."*

"Sounds fun." Remy stepped into the truck and rested her foot on the doorjamb. "Dessert."

A low rumble of laughter teased Remy through the phone. *"Cherry."*

"Pie." Remy's skin was starting to tingle.

"Clit."

"Lick." The sound of short, raspy breaths came through the phone, and Remy knew that Sarah's mind was in the same gutter hers was in. "As in, I need to taste you again. I want to fuck you with my tongue. I want to suck your clit and make you scream my name."

"Wow! I can't remember the last time words got me this hot and bothered." Sarah took several deep breaths, willing the pounding ache in her aroused core away. *"Where are you?"*

"Missouri. Springfield. You?"

"Tulsa." Sarah answered breathily, her heart still pounding.

"Hang on."

Remy's tone was just husky enough to send Sarah's libido into overdrive. It shouldn't affect her this way, but it did. No way someone's voice should send shivers down her spine, but Remy's did. Actually, if just talking to someone could give a person an orgasm, Sarah would bet money that Remy had made hundreds of women come just from saying hello.

Sarah heard papers rustling in the background. "Meet me." Remy said quietly.

There it was again, the flutter in her stomach. *"Where?"* Right now, Remy could say the moon and Sarah would figure out a way to get there.

"Joplin. That's halfway for both of us." Remy's tone was matter—of—fact. She wouldn't take no for an answer, not after three weeks anyway. Her body had a mind of its own, and right now it was telling her if she didn't see Sarah soon, there might be problems.

"Yes." One word, and Sarah's nerves took over. She needed to see Remy, needed to feel her body pressed against hers, wanted another night like before, but she felt the doubt start to feather its way into her subconscious. Would it be that magical again or had it been a fluke? Two times are amazing, but what if the third time the truth comes out. She shook her head. *"I can't wait to see you."*

"Until tonight." Remy's voice was even huskier than before and Sarah could hear the naked longing in her tone. "And, Bonneville?"

"Uh-huh?"

"Don't forget." It was Remy's way of telling her she loved her. Sarah hadn't been able to respond in kind to her earlier proclamation, but Remy still needed her to know, and this was the second best way she knew how to get her meaning across.

Sarah took a deep breath, her heart clenching in her chest. *"I won't…I promise."*

Remy smiled widely. She was one hundred percent, head over heels in love, and by her calculations, a mere three hours from seeing Sarah again. "Until tonight, Bonneville."

She hung up the phone as Carmen made her way back to the truck. Remy couldn't get the shit—eating grin off her face in time to avoid arousing suspicion, so it was no surprise Carmen gave her hell about it.

"Chica, you are smiling like the bear that ate a canary. Que pasa?"

Remy shook her head, laughing out loud. "It's cat."

"Huh? You are smiling about a cat?" Carmen looked confused, which made Remy laugh even louder.

"No, I'm not smiling about a cat. It's the *cat* that ate the canary, not the bear. How on earth would a bear get a hold of a canary?"

"No se, Chica. How would I know? You are the one that keeps talking about a cat." Carmen was glaring by now, and none too happy when Remy could not stop laughing.

When Remy finally got herself under control, she shot Carmen a devilish grin. "Never mind the cat, guess where we are going?"

Carmen's brows furrowed. "Disney World. You know I always wanted to go there, but my momma wouldn't take me. How the hell should I know where we are going?"

Her tone was so sarcastic, Remy couldn't help but laugh. "Joplin."

"Missouri?"

"Si, Chica. I've got a little surprise for you." Remy started the truck and eased it away from the station, a mysterious smile on her face. "Just sit back, drink your Coke and enjoy the ride."

Two and a half hours later, Remy pulled into a Holiday Inn and got out, stretching her long legs. She shut the door and poked her head through the window. "Tell Parker we are at the Holiday Inn on Range Line."

Thirty minutes later, Sarah's battered Chevy pulled into the parking lot, and Remy bounded outside to greet her. Rather than stay in their room, she had stalked the hotel lobby. She pulled Sarah's door open hastily, and her eyes raked over Sarah's body hungrily. She finally met her amused gaze, a guilty smile on her face. "Hey."

"Okay, tell me we aren't playing that game again." Sarah's tone was teasing, but her eyes were dark with hunger. "Besides, you know I'd rather do it with you than talk about it anyway."

Remy's mouth opened and closed several times before she could manage a coherent thought. "I, um, got you guys a room already. I didn't want to take a chance there wouldn't be one by the time you got here."

Parker cleared her throat loudly, her eyes dancing with amusement.

"Oh hey, Parker." Remy didn't even pretend to be embarrassed. They were all adults and clearly all aware of the new situation between her and Sarah. "Carmen's upstairs already. Room 230. Here's the key."

Parker grabbed the key before Remy could even blink and headed towards the hotel. "Guess we won't be seeing them till tomorrow."

"That's okay. I've seen enough of her to last me a while." Sarah popped the trunk and started to grab her bag. Remy took it from her hand, and she caught her scent on the breeze. She felt her knees quiver. Just Remy's scent spiked her blood pressure. *Get a hold of yourself Sarah.* She put some space between them and smiled. "Thanks."

If Remy noticed her withdrawal, she didn't mention it. Nothing was going to ruin her mood today. "Sure. Come on, let's take your bag up and let you get settled."

Sarah nodded and followed Remy into the lobby, her eyes never leaving her tight bottom.

Chapter 22

Remy held the door open, her eyes never leaving Sarah's as she walked in the room. She shut the door and set Sarah's bag on the end of the bed. She tucked her hands in her back pockets and rocked back and forth, unable to pull her gaze away from Sarah's face.

There was an awkward silence between them, the solitude of the room making them uncomfortable. This was the first time they had been alone since the morning of their aborted lovemaking. It was evident in their eyes what they were thinking. A continuation of that morning but neither one was sure how to start it. The only sound in the quiet room was the sound of their quickened breathing.

Remy finally laughed nervously. "I bet you're tired. You want me to give you some privacy so you can relax a bit."

Sarah shook her head from side—to—side, her eyes never leaving Remy's

"Are you hungry?" Remy shuffled nervously. "We could grab some dinner."

"Yes, I'm hungry." Sarah stepped closer, and Remy could feel her breath on her face. "But, not for food."

Before Remy could react, Sarah was ripping her shirt over her head. She felt her pulse quicken and her stomach catch. Before she could move, Sarah captured her lips against hers. Sarah's tongue raked across her lips, seeking entry and when her lips parted, Sarah's tongue darted inside.

Remy's head was swimming. She wasn't used to a woman taking control, and the thought made her immediately wet.

Sarah's hands roamed freely over Remy's naked breasts, arousing her nipples to achingly taut peeks. She broke the kiss. "I can't wait any more. I need to feel you."

Remy could only nod, her body ached to be touched. She started to walk towards the bed, but Sarah pushed her back against the door roughly, her eyes dark pools of desire. She felt Sarah undoing her jeans, and her hand dove into her panties. She needn't worry that she wasn't ready, Sarah was already swirling warm cream over her lips.

"God, you're so fucking wet." Sarah licked her neck hungrily. "You are so fucking sexy. Do you know how crazy you make me?"

Remy shuddered. Sarah's fingers were buried deep inside her. She was talking dirty, and it was making her blood boil. She swallowed loudly, leaning against the door for support. Before long, she moved against Sarah's fingers, bringing them deeper inside her.

"Yeah, that's it baby. Ride my hand, I'm going to fuck you so good." Sarah's mouth was devouring Remy's body. Everywhere she touched was hot and delicious. "You like that, don't you? You like my mouth on you and my fingers inside you." She accentuated each word with a deep stroke inside Remy.

Remy's voice was raspy, and she managed to utter a low moan. She couldn't have answered if she wanted to. The blood had left every other part of her body and pooled around her aroused core. Her clit hammered painfully, and she arched against Sarah's hand, begging for her to assuage her ache.

"Not yet, baby." Sarah withdrew and plunged three fingers inside Remy's swollen core, feeling her contract around her. "Oh god, you're so close. I can feel you quivering around me."

Remy nodded again and dropped her head against the door. Her knees were shaking, and she struggled to stay standing. Her body hovered between pleasure and pain, her arousal so acute now that she thought she might die if she didn't come soon. "Please."

Remy's pleas broke through the haze of desire in Sarah's brain. She quickened her pace and used her hip to increase the pressure of her strokes. Her thumb found Remy's clit and she stroked it deftly.

Remy's moans filled the room as her body arched against Sarah's hand begging for release. Her legs quivered helplessly, and when her orgasm hit, she braced her palms against the door and rode Sarah's hand, feeling wave after wave of pressure ripple through her body. When she finally came back down, she laid her head on Sarah's shoulder and fell into her body. "Oh…my…fucking…God. That was incredible. I like it when you are hungry."

Sarah smiled against her cheek, her fingers swirling over Remy's wet folds teasingly. When Remy groaned and tried to pull away, she had mercy on her. She pulled her dripping fingers out and licked them clean one by one, moaning appreciatively.

Remy blushed. She smiled shyly. Small tremors still shook her, and she wrapped her arms around Sarah to steady herself. She kissed the top of her head and inhaled deeply. "I hope that was just an appetizer."

Sarah chuckled softly. "Don't worry, I think tonight will be a five course dinner." She could feel Remy's heart pounding against her and knew that their hearts were beating in time. She wondered at the twist of fate that had brought them back together, or more appropriately, had never let them part.

She was learning very quickly that she didn't just want Remy in her life, she needed her and that was a scary thought to accept. Oh well, she would just need to figure out a way to deal with it. She knew already that Remy wasn't about to let her get away again. Her only question now was how involved she would let her heart become. So far, she had made Remy believe it was just physical, but she knew there was no way she could keep fooling Remy with that line of reasoning. More importantly, how long would she be able to fool herself? She knew admitting the truth to that answer was going to be the hardest part.

"Penny for your thoughts." Remy's voice broke through her ruminations.

Sarah pulled away and laughed softly. "Nothing too important. Just thinking I might want to take you up on your offer for dinner now."

Remy saw something in her eyes and it made her breath catch. She looked for it again, and just as quickly as it had been in Sarah's eyes, it was gone again. But, no matter, Remy knew what it was. She had seen the same look in her own eyes every time she looked in the mirror. She was in love, and unless she was mistaken, Sarah was too. She also figured Sarah's quietness was a result of still fighting against her heart and the feelings she was having. *Soon, Bonneville. You will realize what I already do.*

She held Sarah at arms' length and smiled. "Pizza okay?"

"Yes." Sarah ran over to grab her purse. "I'm famished now and that sounds awesome."

"Funny, I'm famished too." Remy winked lasciviously. "But, you will need some food for the night I have planned."

She laughed at the look on Sarah's face and grabbed her hand, pulling her out of the room. "Come on. The sooner we eat, the sooner I get dessert."

Sarah tugged against her. "Think we should ask the girls?"

"Nah." Remy shrugged. "C said that as long as it has been since she's been with Parker, I would be lucky to see her before Tuesday. Besides, there's a McDonald's if they get hungry."

Ten minutes later Remy pulled into a spot in front of Mazzio's Italian Eatery. "This okay?"

"Perfect, let's just hope it's not packed." Sarah followed Remy inside. "I think my stomach is about to eat itself."

"Well, tell it to stop. The only eating of any part of your body is going to be by me."

The thought of Remy's mouth on her body got Sarah's libido going again. "Just feed me first and you can have your way with me."

Remy smiled wickedly. "I'll remember you said that."

Sarah wasn't sure what Remy had planned, but the look on her face sent shivers down her spine. "Should I ask?"

"Nope." Remy said a few words to the greeter and two minutes later, they were sitting at a booth in the corner of the restaurant. "Something's are better as a surprise."

"Fine, whatever." Sarah stuck her tongue out at Remy.

"Is that a threat?"

"A promise." Sarah smiled wickedly. Two could play at this game. "I'm picking the pizza then since you obviously have our dessert all lined up."

When the waitress came by their table, Sarah ordered two Cokes and a Four Meat pizza, ignoring the snort that came from across the table.

"You like your meat, huh?"

"Only on pizza. Otherwise, I'm a vagitarian."

Remy's eyes danced mysteriously. "For now."

"Are you planning on letting me in on your little secret?"

"Uh—uh." Remy took a swig of her Coke and smiled innocently. "So, how'd things go for you guys? Catch anything?"

"Nah, the storms weren't biting. That, or I wasn't using a big enough rod."

Remy snorted loudly and she choked down a mouthful of Coke. "You crack me up, Bonneville." Her eyes narrowed thoughtfully. "You sure you don't know about dessert?"

Sarah shook her head. "Not a clue."

Remy reached across the table and covered Sarah's hand with hers. "You are so adorably innocent and sweet."

"Is that a good thing?" Sarah's brow furrowed.

"Only if I'm the one that gets to corrupt you."

Sarah wove her fingers around Remy's. "Especially if you are the one that gets to corrupt me."

The look in Sarah's eyes was a mixture of longing and sweet innocence, and it made Remy's heart thud against her chest.

The waitress interrupted the moment and set a large pie in between the women. "Enjoy."

They fell into friendly banter, and before either one realized it, they had eaten all but two slices of pizza. Remy leaned back in her chair and sighed loudly. "Okay, now I'm stuffed."

Sarah waggled her eyebrows. "As long as you still have room for dessert."

"No worries, darling." Remy leaned forward, capturing Sarah's eyes with hers. "I'll always be hungry for you."

Sarah's breath caught in her throat. The air around them crackled with undisguised desire. Her body thrummed in anticipation, and she pushed her chair back impatiently. "I think we need to go...now."

Remy paid the check and followed Sarah to the car. Her hand found Sarah's leg, and she caressed it softly. She felt Sarah's muscles flex underneath her palm, and she increased the pressure. Her hand slid up possessively, and Sarah's hand covered hers, holding it still.

"You're going to have to stop, or we won't make it out of the car." Sarah warned gently.

Remy held her hand still. "Then I'll wait."

When they got back to the room, the nervousness from earlier was gone, replaced by smoldering desire. What Sarah had started before dinner was going to be continued without the previous urgency. Remy slowly undressed Sarah, and

when she was naked, she laid her down on the bed. She .
kissed her softly, their tongues slowly exploring one
another's mouths.

Every stroke of Remy's tongue made her clit jump, and
before long, she was clawing at Remy's clothing, trying to
get her naked.

Remy's shook her head from side—to—side. "Not yet."
She kissed Sarah on her forehead and smiled reassuringly.
"I'll be right back with your surprise."

Sarah waited anxiously. Whatever it was, all she knew
was she was ready for Remy's touch. She needed her mouth
on her and inside of her. None of her thoughts could have
prepared her for her surprise.

Remy walked towards her completely naked, except for
a strap—on. Sarah sucked in a breath nervously, but her
stomach fluttered wildly. Her eyes dropped to Remy's
surprise. "It's…ahh…it's so big."

Remy lay down next to Sarah, and her hand cupped her
breast. She caressed her nipple with her thumb. "Don't
worry, baby. I'll go slowly. If it's too much, just tell me. We
can stop. Just trust me."

Sarah's body was already reacting to Remy's hand on
her breasts. She could feel wetness between her legs, and she
couldn't deny that the thought of Remy buried deep inside
her made her blood beat faster. She pulled Remy's face
down to hers and kissed her deeply. "I trust you."

Remy's hand roamed over Sarah's body, igniting fires
wherever she touched. She captured Sarah's lips with hers
and their tongues tangled together. Remy slid her hand over
Sarah's hip and down the vee between her legs. She dipped
her finger into Sarah's core and rubbed her juices over her
lips. She pulled her hand away and lifted her body over
Sarah's.

Remy hovered over her, her arms supporting her weight.
Remy's eyes found Sarah's, and she smiled again. "Are you
sure?"

"Yes." Sarah answered without hesitation. She leaned up and kissed Remy softly. Her instincts took over, and she wrapped her hand around Remy's sex and poised it against her wet center. "I want you to make love to me."

Remy's heart burst at her innocent surrender. She slid the tip of her erection into Sarah and waited for her to adjust to her size. Her eyes found Sarah's and the only thing she saw there was love. She lowered her body further, and waited again. Finally, when Sarah had taken her full length, she stilled, their bodies pressed together.

When Sarah nodded, Remy pulled out and slid into her again, her slick juices easing the pressure. The first few minutes, Remy worked inside her slowly, stroking as deep inside Sarah as she could.

Sarah's body opened slowly, and the pleasure in her body outweighed any pain she felt. Soon, she was moving with Remy, their bodies matched in a perfect rhythm. She suddenly knew what Remy had meant earlier when she said it was something she had to try to know how good it was.

Needing release, Sarah wrapped her legs around Remy and pulled her into her body tightly. "Harder please. I need it harder."

Remy arched her head back and braced her arms, burying herself deeper inside Sarah's body. Her hips pounded furiously as Sarah met every stroke with equal fervor. She could feel Sarah's legs shaking around her and knew she was close. Remy leaned forward, rubbing her mons over Sarah's engorged clit.

Sarah's body tightened and when the orgasm hit her, she came off the bed. Pleasure ebbed through her body and shattered her senses. Her legs clenched Remy's hips and held her inside her as she crested and crashed and crested again.

When the orgasm finally let her body go, Sarah fell back against the bed. Her body was limp, and she didn't think she would ever be able to move again. When she was finally able to move, she chuckled softly. "I had no idea *that* was what I was missing. You can surprise me like that all the time."

Remy couldn't help but smile. "I may have one or two more up my sleeve."

"Mmm." Sarah moaned contentedly. "After that, you can do whatever you want."

"I'll remember you said that, Bonneville." Remy slid off of Sarah's body and she stood up. She undid the strap—on and set it in the chair. She slid into the bed and curled her body around Sarah's, her arm wrapped around her softly.

Sarah wriggled her bottom into Remy's core and she moaned softly. "So, umm, you think I might be able to do that to you sometime?"

Remy nuzzled her nose in Sarah's hair, breathing in her fruity shampoo. "I think that could be arranged." Her heart pounded faster. She hadn't ever had a woman ask if they could return the favor and the mere thought of it made her a little crazy.

"Okay. good." Sarah put Remy's hand on her breasts, and she sighed softly. "Hey, Remy?"

"Yeah, Bonneville?"

"Don't forget."

Sarah's voice was almost a whisper, and Remy was sure she imagined the words. It didn't matter though, she didn't need to hear them, she had already felt them.

Chapter 23

Remy knocked on the door softly. She could only imagine as long as it had been since Carmen had seen Parker, that they had been up the majority of the night. She had to knock several more times before a tired, and definitely sated looking, Parker opened the door. She handed Parker a cardboard drink carrier with four large coffees. "Figured you could use the extra caffeine today."

Parker raised her eyebrows amused. "You know me well."

Remy shrugged. "I know, C." She started to walk away then on second thought turned back and smiled at Parker. "You guys better get moving. There's a line of thunderstorms developing over Kansas. Should be here by late afternoon."

Carmen's head popped out over Parker's shoulder, and Remy had to smother a laugh at the *freshly fucked* hair piled high atop her head. "Morning, C. Rough night?"

Carmen patted her hair and smirked. "No more than yours, Chica. Tell me there's something good. We haven't seen a good storm in weeks."

"The same system already dropped a couple of twisters in Minnesota. We may finally get something good."

Parker leaned over and kissed Carmen's cheek. "See, I told you something would come up soon." She held up the

191

drinks and returned Remy's earlier smile. "Thanks for the coffee. Do we have time for breakfast too?"

Remy smiled mischievously. "I fully intend to have breakfast in my room. If you want, we can meet up this afternoon for a late lunch."

Parker's grin was equally lascivious. "I like the way you think."

Remy smiled once more and spun on her heel, thoughts of a late morning breakfast consisting of one Sarah Phillips suddenly making her very hungry.

Several hours later, the four women held burgers in one hand and phones zeroed in on the local radar in their other hand. Remy focused in on a supercell that had developed over Kansas. Further north, a small tornado had already touched down over Topeka. "This is the one right here. Look at the bow echo here at the bottom."

Sarah leaned over her shoulder, breathing in her scent. She resisted the urge to kiss her cheek, instead zeroing in where her finger pointed. "Yeah, definite rotation there. You could be right."

"Could be?" Remy's brow furrowed.

"Yes, Ms. Tate. Could be." Sarah teased. "Contrary to what you think, you can be wrong."

"Humph!" Remy snorted loudly. "Wrong? Name one time."

"Well there was that one time in Little Rock."

Remy glared at Carmen. "That was an honest mistake. Anyone could have made it."

Carmen laughed wickedly. "I didn't."

"Come on guys, let us in on the secret." Sarah pleaded. "Give me something that makes Remy seem less than perfect."

Remy blushed. "Believe me, darlin', I'm far from perfect."

"So, you say." Sarah turned to Carmen. "So, what was it?"

Carmen saw Remy glare and shake her head from side—to—side. Ignoring her silent warning, Carmen leaned across the table. "Let's just say Remy here was about to get down and dirty with a chick she'd picked up in a club when she realized she might come with a little extra baggage."

"You mean packing?" Sarah blushed, her own knowledge of a strap—on was now first hand and thinking of it made her stomach flutter.

"Uh—uh, she was traveling with her own God given parts. Twigs and acorns."

"It's twigs and berries." Remy smiled ruefully. "I totally missed it. Let's just say getting out of that was quite embarrassing."

Sarah laughed out loud and was joined by the others. "I bet. So, I guess you only go for store bought twigs."

"Ahh, yes." Remy rubbed the back of her neck uncomfortably. "And, thank you C, for bringing up that little piece of history that I had conveniently forgotten."

"Anytime, Chica." Carmen shrugged innocently. "I had too. Sarah's under the misguided notion that you are perfect, and I feel like it is my responsibility to set her straight." She dropped her head on Parker's shoulder. "Besides, the only perfect woman here is mine."

Parker blushed wildly. Anyone in the room could tell they were in love. She kissed the top of Carmen's head quickly. "Far from it, but perfection in the eyes of my lover makes me feel like I could hang the moon."

"I think I just threw up a little." Remy rolled her eyes sarcastically. "Do you think you two lovebirds can table your romance for a while and concentrate on the matter at hand?"

Parker's bottom lip jutted out and she pointed at Sarah. "She started it."

"Did not."

"Ladies, please." Remy's voice was stern but her twinkling eyes belied her seriousness. "The storm?"

Sarah and Parker eyed her sheepishly.

"I don't know about you guys, but C and I are going to stay right around here. The storm's tracking this way, and I have a feeling it's going to stir up something crazy."

Sarah agreed readily. "That is if you don't mind Parker and I stealing some of your thunder, so to speak."

Remy shrugged. "If the storm hits like I think it will, there will be plenty of it to go around."

Sarah smiled, and she caught Parker's answering smile out of the corner of her eye. She and Remy had never chased together, and while they wouldn't technically be on the same team, they would at least be in the same vicinity. Hopefully this time, Remy wouldn't do anything stupid like drive straight into the tornado.

"So, it's settled. We need to get moving." Remy had glanced outside and seen the approaching clouds and she knew the storm was close.

They paid the bill and headed out to the parking lot, towards their respective cars. She shot Sarah a look over the hood. "Hey, Bonneville."

Sarah paused, her hand on the open door. She looked over her shoulder at Remy, and the look in her eyes made her breath catch. Her mind flashed to last night, and her heart thudded in her chest. When she spoke, her voice trembled softly. "Yes?"

"Don't forget." Two words, and with them as much feeling as Remy could convey without saying I love you. Her eyes spoke volumes though. She felt the heat that passed between them, and she shivered uncontrollably.

Sarah nodded. "Please be careful."

Remy smiled and threw up her hand in a small wave. She would be careful now. Sarah had asked her to. Danger no longer held a thrill for her. How could it in comparison with the feelings that welled deep within her? What use did she have to fill her life with a disregard for her safety when she was so full of love?

Her need to chase no longer took first place in her life. Carmen had been right. All those years, she had been so focused on her mission, she had missed her life passing her by. Now, she had found a balance, knowing that love had a place, that it could co—exist and make her better.

A loud clap of thunder made her jump. "Shit." Remy jumped into the truck and smiled at Carmen sheepishly. "Sorry."

"Si, Chica." Carmen giggled. "Sitting there waiting for the concrete to dry."

"Paint."

"Que? Paint what?"

"It's paint. Sitting there waiting for the paint to dry, and I wasn't doing that. I was looking at the rather large wall cloud that blew in while you and Parker were giving each other an oral exam in the parking lot."

Carmen snorted loudly. "Like you weren't giving Sarah a serious eye fuck yourself."

Remy nodded guiltily. "Si. I can't help it though."

"So, you know exactly how I feel."

"Yeah, I do." Remy agreed quickly.

"So, what do you say we vamos, so we can get back to where we really want to be?"

Remy started the engine and put the truck in drive. "Good idea."

They followed Sarah's Chevy out of the parking lot, angling towards the southwest corner of town. Remy eyed the building storm. "It's really moving, C. This could be bad."

If the storm continued on the path it was currently following, and it did drop a tornado, the southern portion of Joplin was going to be in trouble. Remy pulled into a clearing just south of the city and stopped. She pulled her camera out and started shooting pictures. "This storm is massive. Look at the rotation."

Carmen nodded in agreement, her eyes scanning the dark clouds above. The wind was starting to blow against them fiercely, and she darted behind the truck for protection. Bits of dirt hit her skin with stinging accuracy, and she blinked rapidly, her eyes filled with dust. "It's getting close, Rem."

"I know. I know." Remy scanned the clouds for several more minutes, her body rigid against the increasing wind. "There! There! See the tail." Her camera shuttered a few more times. "It's growing. This is a strong, strong storm."

They watched as the tail grew larger. A definite twister was taking shape several miles to the west of them.

"Debris! It's down, it's down!" Remy shouted as she threw her camera into the truck and grabbed her cell phone. She dialed quickly. She had to shout over the wind blowing at her back. "There is a tornado just west of the city. We are on 44, just east of Coyote Drive. It's heading straight up the highway."

She ended the call and threw her phone in the truck. Her heart pounded wildly. "We have to move now, C."

Remy drove through the median and headed east towards the city, her eyes on the growing twister behind them. "Shit, C! It's massive, it's massive! This one is bad."

"It's moving so fast." Carmen was hanging out the window, her camera poised on the doorframe. She was glad Remy wasn't going the speed limit, or there would be no way she would be able to hang on.

"Are you getting it?" She heard Carmen shout but her words were lost in the wind. "C? Shit, C!" She leaned over and tugged on her shirt. "Get the fuck inside the truck! C, I'm not kidding." Her hands shook on the wheel, and she slowed the truck quickly.

"What are you doing?" Carmen kneeled on the seat, the camera still out the window. "Keep going."

"No, get inside." Remy was practically yelling. The rain had finally caught up to them, and it hammered loudly on the steel, reverberating through the truck.

Carmen jerked the camera back inside. "Shit! Shit!" She turned around and clicked her seatbelt. "Go, go. We need to stay ahead of it."

Thor's wheels spun out of control. Remy let her foot off the gas and eased the truck up to speed. "Come on, come on, move!"

She passed cars parked along the side of the road as Carmen yelled at them to move. Remy knew they wouldn't hear, and if they did, the more daring ones wouldn't move. It was one thing for them to drive into a tornado and park themselves inside the fast—moving winds in a ten thousand pound truck, it was an entirely different thing for a novice in a three thousand pound car to face off with an EF4 tornado. "Stupid."

They came over a small hill, and the edge of the city came into view. "I'm going to try and stay in front of it, C. Don't let us get lost."

"Si, Chica." Carmen pulled a map of the city up and within moments a dot showing their location popped up. "You can stay on this road for a bit longer. Get off on 71 and go north."

"Back by the hotel?" Remy asked loudly.

"Yep." Carmen waited till they pulled onto 71 before she popped her head back out of the truck and propped the camera back on the roof. The rain had tapered off here, the line of the storm not yet at the outskirts of the city. "Shit, Rem." She shouted into the window. "It's gotta be a mile wide."

Remy's head swept back and forth between the tornado and the road. The streets in the city were more deserted than she had seen them, and she said a silent prayer that it was because the tornado warning had been issued in time. She craned her neck to see over the burgeoning tree line. She could barely see the top of the wedge above the tops of the trees.

A loud bang got her attention. "Wait! Wait!" Carmen shouted loudly, and Remy's breath caught in her chest.

"What?"

Carmen slid back in. "The parking lot, there. It's Parker. Pull over."

Remy cut across two lanes of traffic and pulled into an empty lot. The normally busy strip mall was deserted. Like other small towns, they still closed on Sundays. She grabbed her camera and followed Carmen down the road. Gusts of wind and small droplets of rain were just starting around them, and the tiny drops of water stung the side of her face. She suddenly questioned the sanity of leaving the safety of Thor's ten thousand pound steel cage.

She caught up to Carmen and grabbed her arm. "Come on, C. This is stupid. We need to get back to the truck. Sarah's smart. She'll move."

"She can't." Carmen pulled away, a glare in her eyes. "And, that's Parker out there. I'm not leaving her."

Remy had no choice but to follow her. She saw the hood of the car propped up and knew why Carmen had been adamant to stop. A gust of wind pushed her sideways, and she braced herself to keep from falling over. She put her hand up to shield the side of her face. "What the fuck?"

"No se. That car's a piece of shit anyway." Carmen was barreling down on them, her radar zoned in on Parker.

Sarah ran to meet them. "Oh my god, you saw us."

"C did." She nodded over her shoulder at the storm. "We need to get you guys out of here. Come on." Her nerves were on edge. The tornado was so close now. She could see large bits of debris being hurled around inside it. It had already pulled up trees in its path and leveled several homes. That much was evident.

She grabbed Sarah's hand and pulled her after her. "Come on, Sarah!"

"My stuff, it's in the trunk."

Sarah tried to run back, but Remy grabbed her hand and held on. She shook her head. "No, there's not enough time."

Sarah hesitated, but the look in Remy's eyes made up her mind.

She started running, her heartbeat drowned out by the thundering tornado threatening to overtake them.

Parker and Carmen were just a few steps ahead of them, and Remy pulled Sarah, trying to catch up. The wind suddenly picked up, and Remy's blood pressure spiked. The outer bands of the tornado were right on top of them. She grabbed onto Sarah's arm and held her close. Her eyes watched the skies protectively. Bits of debris swirled overhead, and the truck seemed as though it was miles away, and not the length of a parking lot away.

Remy's head whipped around, her eyes searching for some place to take cover. They would never make it to the truck and the options were slim to nil. A gust of wind slammed them to the ground and pain shot up her arm. She tried to push herself off the ground and her wrist crumpled beneath her weight.

Sarah grabbed her under her arms and pulled her up, her own strength surprising her. "Remy, come on!" She yelled, pulling her along, finally catching up with Parker and Carmen.

Remy cradled her wrist against her chest, the wind making it almost impossible to stand up much less run. She wasn't sure what made her look up, but when she did her blood chilled. A large branch was hurtling right at Carmen and Parker. She had no time to think, just react.

"Look out!" Remy threw herself on top of Carmen and Parker, shoving them to the ground. She felt something slam into her head and her last thought before she blacked out was Sarah.

The next few seconds passed in slow motion. Sarah screamed loudly. She watched the branch hit the back of

Remy's head, ramming it into the pavement as she fell between Carmen and Parker. She fell to her knees, ignoring the pain. "Remy! No!"

Parker heard her yell and rolled over. She grabbed her leg and yelled in pain. She looked down at her leg and her face paled. She felt bile rise in her throat. She wasn't sure what had happened other than when Remy had yelled look out, she turned and when Remy shoved her down, her leg had snapped. The wind whipped around her and pain shot up her leg. Carmen touched her leg and she howled in pain.

Sarah's screams pulled her attention away from her own suffering, and her eyes saw the blood pouring from a gash in the back of Remy's head. Still not comprehending what had happened, she tried to reach Sarah's arm.

Sarah jerked away helplessly. She knelt over Remy's body, her eyes wild. "We need to help her. Please stay with me, Remy. I love you."

"Sarah, I can't move."

Carmen stood up, shielding them both. She knew she needed to remain calm. Sarah was a frantic mess and in no position to think clearly. She grabbed her arm and pulled her up.

Sarah tried to throw her arm off, and Carmen jerked her around, shaking her until her eyes focused on her. There was no time for freaking out. What they needed now was to get out of the direct line of the tornado.

"Look, Sarah. We need to move now!" Carmen nodded towards a store. "Let's get them both over there. We can't stay out here!"

Something in Carmen's words finally got to Sarah. She looked between Remy's motionless body and Parker. "Don't worry, Sarah. Parker, I'm sorry."

Parker nodded. "I know, get Remy to safety. I'm okay."

Carmen directed Sarah to Remy's feet and she grabbed her under her arms. They lifted her up, and bracing themselves against the wind, carried her to the front of the store.

"We need to get inside." Sarah ran over and picked up a rock. She hurled it against the window and shielded her face against the breaking glass. She kicked the shards along the bottom of the window and stepped over the frame. She ran to the door, unlocked it and pulled it open. Carmen pulled Remy inside the building and ran back out into the storm.

The rain had started falling in thick sheets, and hail was starting to cover the parking lot. She skidded to a stop next to Parker and grabbed her hand, hauling her up roughly. Her heart broke at Parker's loud groan. She didn't have time to stop and make sure she was okay. She could see roofs peeling off the buildings just across the street. She wrapped her arm around Parker's waist and helped her hop the last twenty feet to the waiting shelter. She could only pray that they would be protected there.

When they made it inside, she saw a trail of blood along the floor. Sarah had been alert enough to pull Remy away from the windows. She found them huddled in a back corner, Remy's head cradled in Sarah's lap. She helped Parker sit down, careful not to bother her leg more than she needed too. In the small bit of light coming in from the window at the front of the store, she could make out the unnatural angle of Parker's leg and she fought the urge to throw up.

"I'm sorry, Parker."

"Don't be." Parker nodded at Remy. "Is she okay?"

"I don't know. Sarah?"

Sarah lifted her face up, and Parker could see the tears streaming down her cheeks. She stroked Remy's forehead and shook her head. "She has a pulse and she's breathing. But, I can't stop the bleeding. We need to get her help."

Carmen shook her head. "I know, honey, but we can't. Not until the storm's over."

She squeezed Sarah's hand reassuringly. She wanted to tell her she would be okay, but the sound of breaking glass stopped her words. She heard the building groan and shudder. "Oh shit!"

Realization dawned on Sarah, and she lifted Remy's head up and slid her arm underneath it. She rolled her body on top of Remy's and prayed she could keep her safe. She buried her face in Remy's neck and held on as the edge of the roof ripped away loudly. She felt rain pound her back. A thought hit her, and she pushed it to the back of her mind. *Please let the walls stay standing.*

It seemed like an eternity before the howling winds and sickening sounds of buildings being ripped apart were replaced by an eerie silence.

"I think it's over."

Carmen's voice broke the silence, and Sarah lifted her head, brushing wet strands of hair off her face. She could finally feel Remy's breath against her neck now that the tornado had passed. She kissed her lips, thankful that they were still warm. The blood around Remy's head had been washed away by the rain, and Sarah hoped that meant the bleeding had stopped. She pulled off her shirt and tucked it under Remy's head gently.

Sarah pushed herself up. "I'm going to get help. Watch her please." She ran outside and stopped dead in her tracks. She shivered in her tank top. The city was leveled. She swirled around and let out a cry. Aside from the walls dividing the stores and the wall along the backside, the building was gone. She saw piles of rubble where stores once sat. She wasn't sure how the small spot where they had huddled stayed clear, and a small part of her started to believe in miracles. Now, she just needed one more.

She heard sirens, and her eyes searched the streets. A siren meant help, and she knew Remy and Parker needed it. She ran up Range Line Road. The street was littered with debris, and she worried that if an ambulance was close, it wouldn't be able to drive anywhere close to them. She threw up her hand in frustration. "Shit! Come on!"

She heard the rumble of a diesel engine, and she ran around the corner waiving her arms furiously. The ambulance slowed and swerved around her and headed north on Range Line. "Fuck! Are you serious?"

Sarah bent over, trying to catch her breath. The first few residents were starting to venture out in the street. She recognized the same stunned silence she had seen countless times before. She waived them down. "Please. The hospital. Where is it?"

One of the men shook his head and pointed southwest. "It's over a mile from here lady."

"Shit!" She couldn't run there. Suddenly, she realized that getting Remy help wasn't going to be as easy as she thought.

Chapter 24

Sarah headed further up Range Line past the debris littering the streets. She wasn't sure what the rest of the town looked like, but everywhere surrounding her looked like a war zone. She skidded to a stop and stared down at a twisted sign. St John's Express Care. *Please,* she thought.

She stumbled over piles of concrete and rubble to what she thought was the door, or at least what remained of it. She stepped over a broken out glass window and looked around, her eyes adjusting to the unlit building. Obviously, the tornado had knocked out power to this entire section of town.

Surprisingly enough, she saw no one. "Hello?" Her voice echoed off the walls and answered back. Finally adjusted to the darkness inside, she started down a narrow hallway. Outside, she could still hear sirens, and she wondered where they would go since much of the hospital was damaged. "Hello? Is anyone here?"

She rounded a corner and slammed into something hard. She stumbled backwards and almost fell when strong arms righted her.

"Shit! Are you alright?" A man in scrubs held Sarah while she collected herself.

"Yes, I'm fine." She pulled away. "Please. My friend. She is hurt very badly. She needs help."

"Lady, look around you." He spoke the words wearily. "We got more hurt than we can even handle. As it is, they are shuttling everyone to Freeman. This couldn't have hit a worse place. Unless it's life threatening, you're going to have a hard time getting help."

Sarah swore loudly. "She's bleeding from a huge gash in her head. Is that life threatening enough?"

The doctor let out a breath. "Damn, lady." He shook his head wrestling with a decision. "Come on. Follow me." He led her back outside and pulled a cell phone from his scrub pocket. "If I'm lucky enough to get a signal, I'll make sure you get help."

He paced outside waiting for the call to get picked up. "Hello? This is Dr. Patrick, St. John's. I need an ambulance."

"No, not from here." He said with a frown.

Sarah waited impatiently, her body shaking from both fear and frustration. She guessed she'd been gone not more than ten minutes, but given Remy's injury, every passing minute counted. She touched his arm. "Please."

He held up a finger to stop her. "No, large gash to the…"

"Back. It's the back of her head." Sarah's heart was thundering in her chest. She needed to get help to Remy, and she prayed this Dr. Patrick could help her.

"To the back of the head. Bleeding profusely."

He listened. "I know there are more injuries than you can deal with right now. Please, she's lost a lot of blood." He met Sarah's eyes and saw the same fear he had seen in his patients moments before. He put his hand over the receiver. "Where is she?"

Sarah pointed southeast. "A couple blocks over. Just across from the Home Depot. Well, what's left of it."

He took his hand away. "She's down by the Home Depot. Take her to Freeman, same as everyone else."

He ended the call. "Come with me."

Sarah couldn't tell what he wanted, but she didn't want to waste any more time. "I need to get back. What if they come…?"

"Listen. I called, they didn't promise. They just said they would try." He saw her face blanche. "Listen, I'm sorry. It's the best I can do." He started pulling supplies out of a metal cabinet. "Take these."

She took bandages, antiseptic and painkillers. She nodded her thanks and left the way she came, her feet hitting the pavement, covering it in long strides. Moments later, she saw the Home Depot. She ran through the broken door and slid to the floor next to Remy.

"You're back?" Carmen raised her eyes from Remy, who was still motionless on the floor. "She hasn't moved at all. I'm worried about her, Sarah."

Sarah shook her head from side—to—side, silently begging Carmen to be quiet. She was worried too, but she wasn't going to be pessimistic either. Remy was a fighter. If anyone could take a hit like that and come through, it was Remy.

She dropped a couple of pills in Parker's hand. "Here. Take these. Hopefully, it will help with the pain." She saw the green pallor of Parker's face and knew that she would probably rather be knocked out as well. "I'm sorry, Parker."

Parker smiled around the pain. "It's cool, Sarah. It's not your fault. Besides, this will score me some major points with my lady."

Carmen squeezed her hand. "You don't need any more points."

Sarah lifted Remy's head back into her lap and turned her head sideways. She could see dried blood in her hair and the edges of what looked like a very nasty gash. She blinked her eyes tightly, locking the tears away. She was scared and tired. She prayed that Dr. Patrick's request would be answered. She cocked an ear and listened. Sirens still blared out loud, but none seemed to be stopping near them. What if they had driven by and not seeing anyone, drove away without stopping? "Oh shit!"

Carmen's head whipped up. "What?"

"I can't believe I am so stupid. What if they came and didn't know where we were?"

"Who? What if who came?" Carmen tilted Sarah's head up and forced her to look at her. "Sarah, tell me. What if who came?"

"The ambulance." Sarah's voice was frantic again. "You have to go outside and wait. You have to stop them."

"Si, si." Carmen rubbed her arms reassuringly. "When they come, I'll stop them." She hurried outside without another word. The skies were starting to darken as night fell upon the city. Seeing her would be even more difficult in the dark. She arched her eyes to the heavens and crossed herself. Maybe, if she hadn't forgotten her faith all those years ago, she might have been able to call in a favor.

She heard sirens in the distance and prayed for them to get closer. She looked behind her and prayed her friend would get help soon.

Sarah cradled Remy's head in her lap. "Parker, can you move?"

Parker nodded and started to scoot across the floor towards them. She gritted her teeth and swallowed a cry. She couldn't lift her broken leg, and every move she made sent pain radiating up her leg. Whatever pills Sarah had given her either weren't working yet or weren't stronger than over—the—counter ibuprofen. "What do you want me to do?"

Sarah handed her a small bottle of antiseptic. "I'm going to turn her head. I want you to pour the solution over the cut. Maybe we can keep her from getting an infection."

Parker opened the bottle and poured it over the part of the gash she could see. She saw it bubble in Remy's hair and knew it was working. "Enough?"

"I guess, I don't really know." Sarah ripped a bandage open and dabbed at the opening. Fresh blood seeped from the opening. "Shit!" She ripped open the remaining bandages and held them to the wound. They were soaked with blood within seconds. "She's losing blood again. I'm out of ideas."

"Maybe if you sat her up. You know get her head above her heart."

Sarah quirked an eyebrow. "You think that will help?"

Parker shrugged. "It always does on TV."

Sarah propped her up against her chest. "Cross your fingers." She let out a deep breath. Her own fingers were crossed. She couldn't even picture her life without Remy now. Remy had been a part of her life for eight years, and now she was part of her heart. She stroked Remy's cheek.

"They're here!" Carmen yelled through the door. She ran back to them leading two paramedics.

Sarah breathed a sigh of relief. "They here, Rem." She met Carmen's eyes. "Thank you."

"Parker, I'm sorry."

"Stop apologizing, Cuz." She knew that she wouldn't go to the hospital, and she tried to ignore the pain in her own leg. Of the two, Remy was in worse shape, and she didn't begrudge her the trip to the hospital. "I'll just have Carmen piggyback me to the nearest emergency room." She winked at Sarah, hoping to relieve her guilt.

Sarah hugged her quickly, avoiding her leg. She watched the paramedics lift Remy gently on to the gurney. They strapped her on and wheeled her out to the waiting ambulance. Sarah walked beside them the entire time, Remy's hand clasped in hers. "I'm going with her."

"Of course." She stepped into the ambulance and wilted into the seat. She laid her head in her hands and felt her determination crumble. One of the paramedics sat opposite her, checking Remy over. She checked her vitals, listened to her heart, tried to see the cut at the back of her head with little success.

In the artificial light of the ambulance, Sarah studied Remy's face. It was ashen, and her lips were colorless. She could see a spot of blood pooling underneath her head. Her lips trembled. She cursed all the time she had put Remy off, not following her heart. Everything had always been tomorrow, but what if there were no more tomorrows. What if the time they had shared was all they got. She wouldn't accept that, couldn't believe that a few weeks was all she would share with her.

Ignoring the paramedic, she pulled Remy's hand to her chest and leaned over her. "Please, Remy. Stay with me. I just found you again, and I don't want to lose you. I love you, Remy. I love you more than I ever thought possible. Please come back to me."

She could feel the jerks as the driver swerved to avoid debris and maneuvered around fallen buildings, their edifices now in the streets. She had no idea how far they had traveled, when they finally careened to a stop. The doors flew open, and the paramedics pulled Remy from the ambulance with gentle speed. She followed them through automatic doors and past a waiting room full of strangers, every one of them hurt somehow.

The true damage of the storm hit her. Remy had not been its only victim. At least a hundred people sat waiting, and who knows how many had already been seen, or were sent to other hospitals.

"Miss?" The paramedic stopped her. "You need to wait outside."

"But..." Sarah protested. She didn't want to let Remy out of her sight again.

"You will get her back in one piece, I promise."

Sarah forced herself to stop. She watched them wheel her down a long hallway until they turned a corner. The full enormity hit her at that moment. Remy was hurt. Parker was hurt, and probably not high on the list of injuries. Tired and mentally exhausted, she slid down the wall. She pulled her knees to her chest and hugged them, trying to find something of comfort. It wasn't long before the tears started streaming down her face.

Chapter 25

Sarah tilted her head sideways and studied Remy's face. The bruises around her eyes were almost faded. She was still wearing a sling for her sprained wrist. "I don't think it looks so bad. You can barely see it."

Remy rolled her eyes. "Maybe, from the front. Seriously though, the back half of my head is shaved. I feel naked."

Saran chuckled softly and kissed her lips. "Have I told you how cute you are when you worry about your looks?"

"Yes." Remy's face broke into a smile. "But, tell me again."

Sarah leaned over again. "You are so adorable with your shaved head and your sexy white bandage." She accentuated each word with a kiss. She leaned back and studied Remy's face again. "Maybe you should just shave it all off."

Remy's eyes widened, and she ran her good hand through the hair she did have left. "And, get rid of the reason you fell in love with me?"

"You're assuming I love you." Sarah's eyes twinkled. "I think you hit your head harder than you thought."

Remy's face fell then she smiled innocently. "I may have heard that you did."

"Oh yeah?" Sarah watched the emotions play on Remy's face, and she couldn't keep the smile off of her face. "And, who told you that information?"

"Parker might have divulged that little secret. But, I would have found you out eventually."

"What are you accusing me of now?" Parker shuffled into the room, twisted on her crutches and stopped next to Remy's bed. "I can't seem to catch a break lately."

"I'd say you caught quite a break that day." Remy teased.

Parker rolled her eyes. "Funny, Tate. So, how are you?"

"Better. The painkillers at this place are amazing!"

"Yeah, Carmen kept me up to date when I wasn't knocked out myself." Parker shuffled nervously. "Listen, I wanted to thank you for, you know…"

Remy waived her hand dismissively. "You would have done the same thing. Although, this hair would have looked a lot better on you."

Sarah chuckled. "She's having trouble with the whole half head of hair thing she's got going on. I told her she should go ahead and shave it all off."

Parker leaned back and studied her face, a serious expression on her face. "Man, I don't know. You don't really have the face for it."

"Hey." Sarah slapped her arm.

Parker smiled sheepishly. "I'm kidding. I'm sure you would look fine." She added under her breath. "Probably got a funny shaped head, though."

"Honey, be nice." Carmen came in carrying bags of fast food. "Don't mind her. She thinks she's gorgeous. I agree with Sarah. You should shave your head. High and tight. Very hot!"

"Hey!" Parker's lip jutted out.

"Don't worry. I only have eyes for you. Believe me, if we haven't hooked up yet, it's never going to happen. Besides, I'm taken and quite in love."

"Speaking of that, I was just reminding Sarah of her eleventh hour confession to my comatose body."

Sarah's cheeks turned bright red. "If I remember correctly, we were discussing your new haircut. Just think of how easy it will be to take care of when we get back on the road."

"I'm not sure you will be getting on the road anytime soon." Remy's eyes were concerned. "Heard Chevy Chase finally bought it in the storm."

Sarah frowned. "That piece of shit was on its last leg anyway. That tree did us a favor. I have been putting it off, but as soon as Parker is up to speed, we'll be looking for a new ride."

"Eh—hmm." Carmen cleared her throat loudly and nudged Parker.

Parker's brow furrowed. "Now?" She saw Carmen nod.

"What?" Sarah watched the interplay between the two women and wondered if whatever secret they had been hiding for the last week was finally going to come to light.

Parker sighed loudly. "I, uhh, need to talk to you about that. I…I mean we…well we want…" She rubbed the back of her neck uncomfortably, and her eyes pleaded with Carmen.

"What my gorgeous lover is trying to say, and rather ineffectively I might add, is that we are done."

"What!" Sarah and Remy said in unison.

"What do you mean done?" Sarah's eyebrows narrowed and she leveled her gaze at Parker.

Parker's grip on her crutch tightened till her hand was white. "I can't do this anymore, Sarah. After this, I realized I don't have your taste for adventure."

"Me neither." Carmen smiled ruefully. "Listen, boss, I think I want to try something different. We've been doing this a long time."

Remy frowned. "Don't let this accident, and that's what it is, an accident take you away from something you love."

"You love it, Remy. I was just along for the ride."
Carmen threaded her arm through Parker's. "I've given this a
lot of thought, and I know it's the right choice for me. I'm
sorry, Rem. I just don't want to do this anymore."

"What about you, Parker?" Sarah studied her face.
"Have you thought about this, really thought about it? We
make a good team."

"I have, Sarah. Carmen's right. This isn't my life, it's
yours."

Remy shook her head, disbelief on her features. "So,
what are you guys going to do?"

Carmen shrugged. "Not sure, really. Might take a trip
back home."

"To Puerto Rico?"

"Si. I think mi Abuela needs to meet the woman I'm
planning on having children with."

Sarah and Remy swallowed loudly. If Parker was
shocked by the announcement, she didn't show it. In fact,
she looked proud.

"So, that's it?" Sarah pressed. "You're just leaving us?"
It didn't come as much of a surprise to Sarah. When Parker
had joined her after Evan left, she didn't think it would be
for good. More than a season, but Parker wasn't a lifer like
she was.

Parker smiled ruefully. "Pretty much."

"Well, I'll be damned!" Remy slapped her hand on the
bed. "I break your leg, and that's the thanks I get."

"Yeah, man, I'm sorry." Parker searched her face for
approval, and when she saw it, her face broke out into a wide
grin.

"So, Carmen's grandmother, huh?" Remy shook her
head, her eyes twinkling mischievously. "Your broken leg is
going to be a walk in the park compared to meeting her
family."

Carmen punched Remy's good arm. "Quit scaring her,
Chica."

"I'm kidding, they are great." Remy caught Parker's eyes and shook her head from side to side. She lowered her voice so Carmen couldn't hear. "I'm not kidding."

Parker winked and mouthed a silent *I know.* She squeezed Carmen's hand. "Listen, I'm thinking we should get out of here and let the dust settle."

"I think you are right." She met Remy's eyes. "Are we okay, Chica?"

"Si, C." Remy squeezed her hand. "We will always be okay."

They shared tearful hugs and moments later, Sarah and Remy sat in silence, wondering what they would do now. Sarah had no car and no partner, and Remy had no partner and was in no shape to drive.

"Well, I can't say I'm surprised." Remy said after a few minutes. "Carmen stayed longer than I thought she would."

"Hell, I can't believe Parker made it past the first tornado. Had it not been for Carmen, she would have been long gone months ago."

"We'll just blame it on Carmen." Remy picked at a piece of lint. "So, what are you going to do now?"

Sarah shrugged. "Call the station I guess. Beg them for a new set of wheels. You?"

"Not sure." Remy gestured towards her arm. "The season's almost over, and I can't drive anyway. I may just head home and take it easy for a while. I need to find a new spotter anyway, unless…"

Sarah saw the look Remy was giving her, and she was immediately intrigued. "Unless what?"

"It seems as though we both have something the other one needs."

Sarah smiled slyly. "You do have something I need, but I don't think you're going to be up for that for a while."

"That's not what I meant, naughty girl." Remy winked. "And, I'll have you know, I'm a fast healer."

"So, what did you have in mind?" Sarah knew what Remy was suggesting, and she felt her heartbeat quicken. When Parker announced she was leaving, Sarah's first thought was teaming up with Remy. They would be great together, and it would mean seeing her every day instead of every few weeks.

"I think you know." Remy smiled. "So, what do you say? Think you would want to chase with me?"

Sarah shook her head from side—to—side. "Nah, I don't think so. We would never get along spending that much time together."

Remy opened her mouth to protest, but she saw Sarah's eyes twinkling mischievously. "So, you want to do this?"

"Yes." Sarah leaned over Remy and kissed her lips. "But, as lovers and partners first. The other stuff is just our job. I love you." She saw Remy raise her eyebrows. "Yes, I love you. If we do this, I don't want you to forget that I'm your first love. You can't lose focus of us."

Remy studied Sarah's face then smiled. "I won't. I love you, Sarah. I think I have since that first night. I love chasing too. But, you taught me that there's room for both in my heart. Plus, I know if I ever get crazy again, you will always pull me back."

"Then I'm in." Sarah kissed her again. "When you're feeling better, will you do that thing to me again?"

Remy felt the heat start to creep into her face. She saw the storms of emotion swirling in Sarah's eyes, and she knew for the first time in her life, she had found her home.

I have always wanted to write a story about Storm Chasers. I have been fascinated by storms since I was a kid. The 2011 storm season made this book somewhat difficult to write. It was with a heavy heart, that I created a story around two characters with such a dangerous profession. To the real life chasers, you guys are amazing! I can only imagine the fear you face every day. I admire your drive and your desire to research such a destructive force in an effort to gather as much data and prevent as much loss of life as possible.

I'd like to thank Terry and Krista for reading every word I write, and not being afraid to tell me when I need to change something.

And, to the love of my life, thank you for believing in us.

Syd Parker was born in California and resides in Indiana. She loves golfing, biking and spoiling her ten nieces and nephews. She loves to travel and anywhere on the water feels like home. She spends her days toiling away at her day job until she figures out a way to drop the last fifteen strokes to make it on the LPGA tour, although she's totally mastered Tiger Woods Golf on the Wii.

Most days when she's not writing, you will find her on the trails or riding her road bike and praying she doesn't end up in another ditch.

She loves to read a good love story and thoroughly enjoys writing them as well. "It isn't just about writing a story, it's about creating a world and having the reader climb into it, experiencing it in first person. That's my goal...that's why I write."

Check out Syd Parker and Syd Parker Books on Facebook.

14915153R00116

Made in the USA
Lexington, KY
27 April 2012